Jacob tipped up her chin with his finger. 'Want to tell me what happened?'

Fran chewed at her lip. 'I was all set to go in... Well, I was parked out in front, at least...'

'And?'

She swallowed tightly. 'I started to walk up the path when I heard the sirens; I guess it was you on your way to the fire. The fire engine was on your tail, and all the noise...it just got to me. I panicked—*really* panicked. I thought I was going to pass out.'

'You poor kid,' he said gently. Jacob put his hands on her shoulders. 'Have you had panic attacks before?'

'Yes...' Her cheeks went bright red. 'Everyone expects doctors to be able to cope with anything. We see blood and gore and death and serious injury all the time. But I just can't seem to walk into a hospital without breaking out in a cold sweat.'

He stepped back and took her by the shoulders again. 'What if I come with you the first couple of times? Would that help?'

She looked up at him in wonder. 'You would do that?'

'I'll try not to make it too obvious,' he said. 'I can come and go, depending on how you are coping.'

'But what will people think of you being there like some sort of bodyguard?' she asked.

Jacob picked up her h
middle
Fran. N
for now.

Dear Reader

One of the greatest privileges I have experienced as a published author is to be asked to be part of the Heart Foundation in Hobart. Each year a fundraising ball is held in June, and it is Hobart's premier event.

A couple of years ago I was asked to be part of the silent auction, donating a book dedication and/or the use of a person's name as an upcoming character. HER MAN OF HONOUR was that award-winning book—which was, of course, a great thrill.

In 2008 a lovely reader won the bid for the chance to have her name used in one of my books. While I have used her name, the character is not based on her in any other way, and everything else is the work of my imagination and was in no way influenced by a real person. Any resemblance to actual persons, living or dead, business establishments, events or locales is entirely coincidental.

I hope you enjoy THE DOCTOR'S REBEL KNIGHT, for I certainly loved writing it, and am once again delighted to be a part of the Heart Foundation's work in Tasmania.

Melanie

THE DOCTOR'S REBEL KNIGHT

BY
MELANIE MILBURNE

MILLS & BOON

All the characters in this book have no existence outside the imagination of the author, and have no relation whatsoever to anyone bearing the same name or names. They are not even distantly inspired by any individual known or unknown to the author, and all the incidents are pure invention.

First published in Great Britain 2009
Paperback edition 2010
Harlequin Mills & Boon Limited,
Eton House, 18-24 Paradise Road, Richmond, Surrey TW9 1SR

© Melanie Milburne 2009

ISBN: 978 0 263 87326 9

Harlequin Mills & Boon policy is to use papers that are natural, renewable and recyclable products and made from wood grown in sustainable forests. The logging and manufacturing process conform to the legal environmental regulations of the country of origin.

Printed and bound in Spain
by Litografia Rosés, S.A., Barcelona

Melanie Milburne says: 'I am married to a surgeon, Steve, and have two gorgeous sons, Paul and Phil. I live in Hobart, Tasmania, where I enjoy an active life as a long-distance runner and a nationally ranked top ten Master's swimmer. I also have a Master's Degree in Education, but my children totally turned me off the idea of teaching! When not running or swimming I write, and when I'm not doing all of the above I'm reading. And if someone could invent a way for me to read during a four-kilometre swim I'd be even happier!'

Recent titles by the same author:

Medical™ Romance
TOP-NOTCH DOC, OUTBACK BRIDE
SINGLE DAD SEEKS A WIFE
    (*Brides of Penhally Bay*)
THE SURGEON BOSS'S BRIDE

Did you know that Melanie also writes for Modern™ Romance? Her stories have her trademark drama and passion, with the added promise of sexy Mediterranean heroes and all the glamour of Modern™ Romance!

Modern™ Romance
THE FUTURE KING'S LOVE-CHILD
    (*The Royal House of Karedes*)
BOUND BY THE MARCOLINI DIAMONDS

Next month, look out for Melanie's Modern™ Romance
CASTELLANO'S MISTRESS OF REVENGE

CHAPTER ONE

'I ABSOLUTELY loathe going to the beach with you,' Carolyn Atkins grumbled with a rueful grin. 'Compared to you, I don't just look like the side of a house, I look like the whole damn street.'

Fran smiled softly at her older sister. 'Well, you would go and get yourself pregnant with twins. That was just asking for trouble, if you ask me.'

Carolyn rubbed her hand over the generous swell of her abdomen, a slight frown starting to pull at her brow. 'I know…but I would feel a lot happier if we had a permanent doctor in town right now.'

'Please, Caro,' Fran said, a scowl swiftly replacing her smile as she clipped Rufus back on his lead. 'We've been through this every day since I arrived. I'm not cut out to be a doctor now. Maybe I never was in the first place.'

'That's total rubbish, Fran,' Caro said as she dusted the sand off her slip-on shoes. 'You were fabulous at your job. You loved it. You were a borderline workaholic, for pity's sake. It was all you could talk about until—'

'Yes, well, that was then and this is now,' Fran said quickly, giving her beach towel a rough shake. 'I want to forget about it while I'm here. I'm supposed to be having a holiday before you have the babies, remember?'

Caro's shoulders went down on a sigh. 'Honey, I'm worried about you. I know you don't want to talk about what happened, but don't you think it might help you move on better if you discuss it just a little bit?'

Fran picked up the bottle of sunscreen and wiped the sand off it with a corner of her towel before she said, 'For your information, Carolyn, recent studies have shown that people who received post-trauma counselling were no better off than those who had been given none. In fact, there was even some suggestion those who received the counselling were worse off—they got more post-traumatic stress symptoms.'

Caro screwed up her mouth in a wry fashion as she fondled her dog's floppy ears. 'You might not want to be a doctor any more but you obviously still keep up to date. That sounded as if you just read it from the latest medical journal.'

Fran slung her beach bag over her shoulder as they started up the sand back to the house with Rufus, who had a piece of driftwood in his mouth in the hope one of them would throw it just one more time. 'I need this time here away from it all, Caro,' she said in a heavy voice. 'It's not just about the…the incident. Breaking up with Anton was so unexpected. I feel such a fool for not seeing that coming.' It wasn't quite the truth but Fran was so tired of being badgered by her friends and family about her decision to leave medicine.

Caro stopped halfway up the path, seemingly to catch her breath, although Fran suspected she had done it for the sake of her damaged leg. It had been weeks now since the cast had come off and her limp was no better. She tried to disguise it as much as she could but there were days when it ached unbearably.

Today was one of those days.

'Honey, I hate to be the one to say this but I never really thought he was the one for you, as in The One,' Caro said. 'And I know for a fact Mum and Dad felt the same. You only went out…what, once a month, wasn't it?'

Fran tightened her mouth as she held her sister's gaze. 'It's not that I was in love with him or anything but do you have any idea of how I feel now he's shacked up with his pregnant radiologist lover?'

Caro pushed her tongue into her right cheek for a moment. 'Well, let's hope she sees through him sooner than you did,' she said as she started up the path again. 'She ought to, being a radiologist and all.'

In spite of the blow to her pride over Anton's rejection, Fran couldn't hold back a small smile as she helped her sister over the rough steps to the top. Caro's dry sense of humour had often helped her over the last few months. The irony was she had always been the happy-go-lucky one with a ready smile in the past, but now she was…well…realistic. Three years working in the department of emergency medicine had seen to that, and the last three months in particular.

'Oh, darn it,' Caro said as she opened the fridge once they were inside the house. 'I forgot to get more milk and that strawberry yogurt I love. I swear it's pregnancy hormones or something. I keep forgetting the simplest things.'

Fran picked up her purse. 'You stay here and have a nap while I pick them up,' she said. 'There are a couple of things I want from the store in any case.'

'Are you sure you're not too tired?' Caro's gaze dipped briefly to Fran's leg.

Fran made a show of searching for her keys rather than see the pity in her sister's eyes. 'I am not the least bit tired,' she said, and once the keys were in her hand she pasted a bright smile on her face. 'I might even stop for a coffee at that little café you pointed out the other day.'

Caro's face twisted in disgust. 'Ew, coffee. Don't mention the word. I can't believe that was the first thing that turned my stomach. I used to be a five-a-day drinker before I got pregnant.'

This time Fran's smile was genuine. 'I'll bring you back something you do crave, like chocolate, OK?'

Caro beamed. 'You're a honey.'

The drive into the tiny town of Pelican Bay was as picturesque as any Fran had been on, even though she had travelled around most of Australia and had gone on several trips abroad. The deep turquoise of the bay fringed by the icing-sugar-white sandy beach never failed to make her breath catch in her chest. The deeply forested grey-green hills that were the town's majestic backdrop added to the area's exquisite beauty.

Unlike the busy and crowded resort towns and fishing ports further up and down the coast, Pelican Bay had somehow retained its atmosphere of old-world charm. It had a village-like feel. Here people didn't walk past you without making eye contact; instead, they stopped and talked about the weather or where the fish were biting—everyday, inconsequential things that made you feel a part of the community even if you were just visiting for a short period. Now that she was here, Fran wondered why she hadn't visited more often. But, then, as Caro had mentioned earlier, Fran's work had always come first—she had lived for work, not worked to live.

The general store on the main street was exactly that: general. It had everything from fishing bait to locally grown fresh basil. The shelves were stacked with well-known city brands but also local goods, such as home-made preserves and chutneys and relishes. Every Friday there was a cake stall, where home-baked goodies were sold to raise funds for the local primary school where Caro's husband Nick was one of only three teachers.

Once Fran had made her purchases and exchanged more than a few words with seventy-year-old Beryl Hadley behind the cash register, she made her way back out to her car. After the old-fashioned and yet surprisingly efficient air-conditioning inside the store, the heat of the late October afternoon was like being slapped across the face with a hot, wet towel. In what had seemed just a few minutes, some angry bruise-coloured clouds had gathered in a brooding huddle over the hills, casting a shadow over the bay that was as dark as it was menacing.

The gathering storm had whipped up the water of the bay into thousands of galloping white horses, each one grabbing at the bit to get to the shore first. Even the gum trees lining each side of the road were almost doubling over as the wind thrashed at their spindly limbs, arching their spines and making them creak and groan.

Halfway back to Caro and Nick's house the rain started. At first it was just a few plops on the windscreen, but within seconds it became a wind-driven downpour. Fran tried to keep track of the winding road but it was like looking at everything through an almost opaque curtain.

She slowed down to take the next bend but a large black and chrome motorbike suddenly appeared from a side road. She slammed on the brakes, her heart juddering to a stop as the stability control device on her car prevented her from going into a tailspin.

The bike and its rider somehow managed to stay upright, although Fran watched with saucer-wide eyes as it did a slow-motion spin, round and round until it came to a shuddering stop, facing her like a sleek black wolf staring down its prey.

Fran's fingers were so tightly clenched around the steering wheel she had to unlock them one by one, her heart still pumping so hard and so fast she saw bright dots like miniature diamonds darting past her eyes. There was a roaring in her ears and her stomach felt like it had been scraped out with a super-sized soup-spoon, the hollow, sinking feeling making her feel jittery and nauseous. She was shaking all over, a fine sheen of perspiration already trickling down between her breasts and between her shoulder blades as adrenalin continued to surge through her.

She watched as the motorcyclist swung one long leg over his bike and pushed it to the side of the road, the pelting rain bouncing off his head-to-foot black leather gear like small pebbles thrown at the pavement.

Fran felt her fear switch places with anger. She wasn't going to wait for him to come to her. She moved her car off the road and, unclipping her seat belt, shoved her door open and went stomping…well, not quite stomping, more a firm right step and then a sort of left leg drag towards him.

'What the hell do you think you were doing?' she shouted above the roar of the rain and the whipping wind. 'You could have killed us both!'

The man didn't remove his helmet. Instead, he lifted the visor to reveal startlingly ice-blue eyes, the outer rims sur-rounded by a much darker blue, as if someone had taken a felt-tip marker and carefully outlined his irises. His eyes were fringed with ink-black thick lashes, and from what Fran could see of the length of his strong, forceful-looking nose, it looked like it had been broken at least once.

'You must have been taking that bend way too fast,' he said, 'otherwise I would have seen you.'

Fran frowned at him in fury, her fists in tight knots at her sides. '*I* had right of way. *You* were the one who should have slowed down.' She quickly glanced at the side road, looking for a stop sign to add weight to her argument, but there was none.

The man must have seen her glance as he said, 'The give-way sign was knocked down a couple of months ago by a drunk driver. It hasn't been replaced yet.'

Fran elevated her chin. 'So you should have at least paused to check if anyone was coming. This is a main road and it has right of way over T-intersections.'

Those startling blue eyes held hers in a challenging duel. 'I did pause and check and there was no one coming when I came out,' he said. He waited a beat before adding, 'What speed were you travelling at?'

Fran put her hands on her hips, inwardly grimacing at how wet her cotton sundress was. 'I was driving to the conditions, not the limit,' she said, practically repeating verbatim a road-safety campaign orchestrated by the police force across Australia to reduce the number of fatalities on the roads.

Although she couldn't see his mouth, she suspected he was smiling. Not a friendly, nice-to-meet-you smile, more a mocking you're-a-lady-driver-and-don't-know-what-you're-doing sort of smile. Maybe it wasn't a smile at all, she decided. It was probably more of a smirk. The sardonic glint in his eyes made her blood go from simmering to a blistering boil. She had met so many like him during her time in A and E. Men who think they are bullet-proof, hogging the road, taking unnecessary risks and endangering innocent, rule-abiding citizens.

It was hard to guess his age, although Fran suspected he was a year or two over thirty. His voice was deep and what she could see of his skin was tanned and it had been at least eighteen hours since it had last seen a razor. His eyes had fine lines around them, but whether they were from frequent laughter or frowning she couldn't quite tell. He carried himself with arrogant authority, which was another thing that annoyed her. The way he was standing towering over her with his feet slightly apart, his arms folded across his broad chest and his eyes trained on her, made her feel as if *she* was in the wrong.

'I noticed you limping,' he said, glancing at her left leg, a measure of concern entering his tone. 'Did you sustain that injury just then in avoiding a collision?'

Fran tightened her mouth. 'I am not injured, no thanks to you. My leg is…' She paused over the choice of word. 'Was broken a few months ago.'

'Are you new in town?' he asked, bringing his eyes back to hers, his gaze intent and steady and probing.

Too steady.

Too intent.

Far too probing.

Fran blinked the rain out of her eyes and frowned at him. 'Excuse me?'

'I haven't seen you around before. Are you passing through or staying at the bay?'

Fran licked the droplets of moisture off her lips, deciding she wasn't going to give him any personal information about herself. Instead, what she was going to do was report him to the local police for dangerous driving. The town was currently without a doctor. If there had been a collision between them it could have been disastrous. As it was, they had been standing here for the last few minutes without another car passing by. Who knew how long it might have been before someone came along to help if one or both of them had been seriously injured?

'I'm…er…passing through,' she said, which was almost true, she decided. She was staying three months, two before Caro travelled to Wollongong Hospital to have the babies and the month after to help her get into a routine. After that Fran had to decide what to do with the rest of her life. As far as she was concerned, the longer she could put off that decision the better.

The man flipped his visor back down. 'I'm sorry if I caused you a bit of a scare but, as I said, I didn't see you.'

Fran didn't think much of his apology. It certainly hadn't sounded all that sincere. In fact, his whole demeanour seemed to communicate he couldn't wait to get on his way again. She straightened her shoulders, wincing as droplets of rain ran down the back of her neck. 'You think an offhand apology is enough?' she asked. 'Do you realise some people—the ones who don't get killed, that is—have to live for the rest of their lives with serious injuries or disabilities after accidents like you very nearly caused?'

'If you're a stranger to these roads you need to take extra care,' he said, 'especially during a sudden storm like this.'

'Did you even hear what I said?' Fran asked, still glaring at him.

He strode over to his bike and, throwing one leg over, kicked down the stand, before starting the engine with a throaty roar. 'Sorry I can't hang about and discuss the weather with you but I need to be somewhere. See you around.'

Fran narrowed her eyes as she tried to memorise his registration number through the pouring rain, still fuming as he drove off towards town without so much as a wave. She stomped or rather limped back to her car, dripping wet and steaming with anger. She sat behind the wheel for a minute or two as she waited for the downpour to ease. She thought about calling Caro on her mobile but decided against it. There was no point worrying her sister when it would only take a few extra minutes to drive back to town and file a dangerous driving complaint. In any case Caro thought she was going to stop for a coffee, which would have taken much the same amount of time.

The police station was just down from the general store and like many country stations it had previously been a weatherboard cottage built by one of the early pioneers. The front entrance led to a small reception area currently attended by a young constable who looked to Fran as if he should have still been at school. She suddenly felt every one of her twenty-nine years as she approached the desk.

'Can I help you?' the young ginger-haired and freckled constable asked with a helpful smile.

Fran tucked a wet tendril of hair behind her right ear. 'I would like to make a complaint about a dangerous driver,' she said. 'He almost caused a serious accident just out of town.'

The constable reached for an official-looking form. 'Right,' he said, unclicking his pen. 'Can you describe the vehicle?'

'Yes, it was a motorbike,' she answered.

'Would you happen to know the make?'

Fran rolled her lips together. 'Um…no, but it was black and silver…I mean…er…chrome.'

The young man stopped scribbling to look up at her. 'What about the registration number? Did you happen to see that?'

Fran frowned as she tried to remember. 'I should have written it down. I'll remember it in a moment... Let me see...there was a V in it, I think, or it might have been a W. It was raining so hard I couldn't really see the numbers but there was a six in there somewhere...' Her frown deepened. 'Actually, it could have been a nine.'

'What about the driver?' the constable asked with a deadpan face. 'Did he stop?'

'Yes, he did,' she said with a huffy look as she crossed her arms over her chest. 'He made a paltry apology and got back on his bike and drove off towards town.'

'So you weren't hurt or your car damaged or anything?' he asked with the same deadpan expression.

'No, but that's not the point,' Fran said. 'This town is currently without a doctor. Can you imagine what would have happened if there *had* been a collision?'

The constable nodded grimly and resumed his scribbling. 'I'll file a report to see if we can find this guy and issue him with a warning,' he said, and then, looking up again, asked, 'Would you be able to recognise him if you saw him again?'

Fran chewed at her lip. 'We-ll...he was sort of covered... you know...in black leather, all over, boots and all. He didn't take his helmet off, he just lifted the visor, but I would definitely recognise his eyes again.'

The constable lifted his gingery brows. 'What colour were they?'

Fran unfolded her arms. 'Blue,' she said with authority in her tone. 'An icy shade of blue. Sort of like the underside of a glacier. But they had a darker blue around the edges.'

There was a strange little silence.

'Is there something wrong?' she asked.

The young constable's eyes contained a hint of amusement. 'Maybe I should get my superior, Sergeant Hawke, to deal with this,' he said, clearly trying his best not to crack a smile.

Fran pursed her lips. 'I would definitely like to speak to him if he can do something about this irresponsible motor-cyclist who is putting innocent people's lives at risk with his inconsiderate behaviour. Is he here now?'

The constable cleared his throat in a manner that suggested he was trying to disguise a chuckle. 'Yes,' he said. 'He came in a few minutes ago.' He reached for an intercom button on the reception desk and leaned forward to speak into it. 'Sarg? There's a young lady here to see you.' After a moment he looked up at Fran and asked, 'Er…your name, miss?'

Fran flicked her long wet hair back behind her shoulders. 'It's not Miss, it's Doctor, actually,' she said, only because it was true in theory and on paper, if not currently in practice. 'Dr Frances Nin.'

The constable relayed the information to his superior and then got to his feet to direct Fran to the door down the narrow hall, still with that hint of a smile lurking about his too-young-to-be-taken-seriously-as-a-cop mouth. 'Sergeant Jacob Hawke will see you now.'

As Fran made her way to the door marked with the officer's name she suddenly realised how soaked through her clothes and hair were. Just before she raised her hand to knock on the door she glanced down at herself and realised her sodden sundress was practically see-through. She could clearly see the outline of her yellow and pink bikini, which was fine when one was on a remote beach with one's sister, but hardly appropriate attire when one was reporting an incident of the gravity of this to a senior officer of the N.S.W. police force.

She considered turning around and hot-footing it out of the building without formally lodging the complaint, but then she remembered one of the trauma cases she had assessed in A and E a few months before she had quit. A young female driver of only twenty-two had been run off the road by a speeding motorcyclist and as a result had ended up a paraplegic. Her career as a ballet dancer had ended in a matter of four or five seconds, not only destroying her dreams but taking the life of her equally young and hope-filled passenger.

Fran had dealt with the relatives and friends of the two young victims with the training that had been drummed into her, but the human, deeply feeling part of her had lain awake many a night ever since, thinking of how unjust life was, how the ones at fault so often got off with barely a rap over the knuckles. A fine, a licence suspension or even a short prison sentence was never going to bring an innocent victim back to life, and it was never going to console the grieving relatives.

Never.

Fran took a deep breath and raised her hand to knock on the door and then listened as strong, even strides approached the door before it opened.

Then she felt her jaw drop. She had never really felt that before. Jaws didn't really drop, at least not in medical terms. Mouths opened in shock and surprise, eyes flared or bulged, jaws didn't actually drop.

But hers did this time.

Fran stared at him, her mouth hanging open, her eyes taking in his features in one goggle-eyed look. Without the cover of his shiny black helmet she could see he was in the category of heart-breakingly gorgeous, with olive skin, a sharply chiselled jaw that was still liberally peppered with stubble and a sensually sculpted mouth that she suspected had wreaked havoc on many a female mouth in its time, which according to her rough calculations was about thirty-two or thirty-three years.

His blue eyes—those glacier-blue eyes—were centred on hers, making her heart skip in her chest.

'*You!*' she gasped, barely able to pull in a breath to give the word the force she had intended to deliver.

'Dr Nin,' he said with a movement of his lips that indicated mockery. 'And here I was thinking we had no doctor in our midst. Welcome to Pelican Bay.'

'I am not practising at the moment,' she said with chilly emphasis. 'I'm on leave.'

She watched as his raised brow made a perfect arc over one of his eyes. 'Have you been warned you are likely to be on a busman's holiday while you are in town, Dr Nin?' he asked.

Fran set her mouth. 'When I say I am on holiday, I mean it, Sergeant…er…Wolf.'

He gave her another movement of his lips that didn't even come within a whisker of a smile. 'Hawke,' he corrected her. 'Jacob Hawke.'

Fran was annoyed with herself for blushing. She couldn't remember the last time she had blushed. She had dealt with naked men's bodies ever since she had started med school but for some reason the fully clothed, black leather coated body of Sergeant Jacob Hawke made her flush inside and out. In fact, she could feel every hair on her blonde head lifting as if each one was trying to get away from the blast of warmth his presence induced. And it was a blood-heating presence without a doubt. She felt the rush of hot blood in her veins, the electric charge of tension just sharing the same air he breathed.

'Would you like to come into my office?' he asked, holding the door open for her, although she thought the invitation lacked enthusiasm.

Fran knew she would look a fool if she turned on her one good heel and left. She also knew she could end up looking an even bigger fool by staying and saying her piece. But the scare she'd had made her fight response win over her flight one, and, taking a breath that barely inflated her lungs, she stepped past him into his office.

'Take a seat,' he said, and moved around to the other side of his desk.

Fran sat on the hard plastic chair, her eyes scanning his desk for any clues to his personality. She decided in the end he wasn't super-neat but neither was he untidy and disorganised—he was busy.

There was a photo frame next to his computer but she couldn't see the subject of the photo it contained as it faced him, not her. There was a glass paperweight pinning down some papers, containing a dandelion puff inside. She found herself staring at it, marvelling at the way it had been captured there, its fragility permanently protected by its spherical armour.

Fran became aware of the fact he was still standing, again giving her the impression he was not intending this interview to last very long. She met his eyes and felt another wave of colour wash over her face.

'So, you're Carolyn Atkins's sister,' he said, folding his arms across his chest as he leaned back against the filing cabinet. 'You don't look much like her.'

Fran felt her back come up against the hard spine of the plastic chair. 'Is that a crime?' she asked. She had spent most of her life being compared to her beautiful sister and consistently falling short. The events of the last few months hadn't helped her confidence one little bit, which made his comment all the more stinging.

His mouth lifted at one corner but she couldn't tell if it was a smile or a smirk, but she suspected it was something in between. 'Constable Jeffrey informs me you would like to lodge a dangerous driving complaint,' he said. 'I take it that would be against me.'

She raised her chin. 'I realise you're a cop but that doesn't mean you can drive like a maniac,' she said. 'Besides, you weren't in police uniform or on a police bike or official vehicle, neither, as far as I could see, were you travelling to an emergency.'

Even though he didn't move a muscle, his eyes turned from ice to stone. 'Dr Nin,' he said, deliberately pausing before he continued, 'I accept that you were frightened by a near collision but the conditions were hazardous and it is my belief you were travelling a little too fast for them.'

Fran could feel her anger stiffening every bone in her body. She got to her feet indignantly, wincing slightly as her leg protested. 'So it's my fault, is it?' she asked, glaring at him. 'What about you? Weren't you driving a little too fast for them too, or don't the same rules apply to you that apply to everyone else?'

He continued to hold her look for several seconds before he unfolded his arms and pushed himself away from the filing cabinet. 'For your information, Dr Nin, I *was* responding to an emergency,' he said. 'Now, if you will excuse me, I need to tidy up some things here before I leave for Sydney. I have some urgent business to see to there.'

Fran wondered if he was telling the truth or fobbing her off. After all, there had been no witnesses to their 'near collision', as he called it. It was his word against hers, and she knew enough about cops to know how they stuck together, covering each other's backs if the need arose.

She slung her handbag over her shoulder and, fixing him with an I-am-not-going-to-take-this-lying-down look, turned and left his office, closing the door behind her with a sharp click.

Jacob dragged a hand through his hair once she had gone, his eyes going to the photo frame on his desk. His chest still felt as if someone had bludgeoned him with the blunt end of a pylon.

He was the only one left now.

It was weird to think of himself as an orphan.

He picked up his helmet and keys. It wouldn't matter if he drove like a Motor GP driver now, it was too late to say goodbye.

Just like the last time.

CHAPTER TWO

'WHAT on earth took you so long?' Caro asked as soon as Fran came in. The rain was still pelting down outside. 'I was worried about you. Did you get caught up in the storm? Apparently there are powerlines down everywhere. I just heard it on the radio. Rufus is hiding under my bed.'

'Yes, it's certainly a bit wild out there,' Fran said as she slipped off her soaked sandals.

Caro tilted her head. 'Are you OK? You look a little flushed.'

'I'm fine,' Fran said, grimacing as she pulled her wet dress away from her chest. 'I just had a little run-in with one of the locals.'

Caro's finely arched brows disappeared under her fringe. 'Which one?' she asked.

'One of the cops,' Fran said, scowling as her sister handed her a towel. 'What happened to that nice grandfatherly sergeant that used to be here before?'

'Jim Robbins?' Caro said. 'He retired a few months back and moved to Lakes Entrance with his wife so they could be closer to their grandkids. There are a couple of new cops now, including a rather gorgeous replacement for Jim...

Uh-oh…' Caro grimaced at her sister's expression. 'So what happened? Did he book you for speeding or something?'

Fran rolled her eyes. 'Now, that's irony for you,' she said. '*He* was the one speeding and he failed to give way but tried to make it look like *my* fault. He's so arrogant.' Fran gave a toss of her head. 'Sergeant Jacob Hawke has superior attitude written all over him.'

'Sergeant Jacob Hawke has got hot, single, currently available male written all over him,' Caro said with a sparkle in her eyes. 'Maybe you should kiss and make up, considering the man-drought and all.'

Fran gave her a withering look. 'I may be single and staring down the barrel of thirty, but I am not desperate.'

'You didn't find him attractive?'

'I found him annoying.'

'But still attractive, right?'

Fran pursed her lips for a beat or two. 'He's got unusually blue eyes, I'll give him that.'

'What about his body?' Caro asked. 'He works out big time. I've heard he's got his own gym set up at his house.'

'I didn't really notice his body,' Fran lied. 'In any case, he was dressed from head to foot in black leather.'

Caro grasped at her chest in a theatrical manner. 'Be still, my heart.'

Fran couldn't help laughing. 'Don't be such a goose. I'm going to have a shower. Is Nick back yet?'

'No, he's got a parents' and friends' meeting so he said he'd stay at school and do some marking until then. We can have a girls' night. Be a honey and paint my toenails for me? I can't reach them any more.'

Fran handed her sister the damp towel. 'It's a date.'

* * *

Fran was taking Rufus for a walk along the beach ten days later when she saw a male figure jogging in the distance. Her first response was to freeze. She felt the knocking of her heart that reminded her she was alone on a beach with an unidentified man coming towards her. Rufus, as if sensing her alarm, looked up at her with a doggy grin and barked before loping off, his plumy tail wagging enthusiastically as he raced towards the jogger.

'Rufus!' she called, trying to keep up. 'Here, boy! *Rufus!*'

The dog loped on regardless and Fran watched as the runner stopped to bend down to give the dog a ruffle of his ears. The man was dressed in running shorts and trainers but his tanned chest was bare, looking as magnificently male as it was possible to look outside a photo shoot, Fran thought.

She breathed out a sigh of relief as she saw the man's response to the dog. Some people were not 'dog people' and didn't take too kindly to an out-of-control mutt like Rufus bombarding them with sloppy kisses and wet tail slaps. Clearly this man adored canine company and obviously knew Rufus personally, which made her feel better about being alone. She watched as he picked up a bit of driftwood and threw it into the sea. Rufus charged off after it and the man continued jogging up the beach.

As he came closer Fran felt her face colour up and it had absolutely nothing to do with the warmth of the sun.

'Dr Nin,' Sergeant Hawke said as he changed gait to a long easy stride, with Rufus at his side, his doggy tongue lolling out in exhaustion.

When he came to a stop in front of her Fran felt his gaze run over her assessingly, taking in her sarong-clad figure. She wished she had put on something a little less revealing but she hadn't seen a soul on the beach for the past week. In fact, over the last few days she had she had just started to feel she could relax her guard a little bit, not having to worry about people and how they viewed her. She hated people staring at the scar on her leg. Her sarong was fairly sheer but thankfully not *that* sheer.

'Sergeant Hawke,' she said, unable to kept the chill from her tone even though her body felt blisteringly hot.

'Nice day for a walk,' he said, reaching down to toss the stick for Rufus again.

Fran couldn't help noticing the way his biceps bulged as he threw the stick. He was in perfect physical condition, muscular and toned with not a gram of non-functional flesh—as Caro would call it—on his frame. His skin was a deep olive, covered now with a glistening layer of perspiration from hard physical exercise. His shoulders were broad, his waist and hips lean, so lean she could see every contour of his external oblique muscle above his hips. *Stop staring at his groin*, she chided herself, and quickly brought her eyes up to his.

She suddenly realised it was her turn to say something. 'Um…yes…Rufus likes a lot of exercise.'

Jacob Hawke gave her his first smile. Well, strictly speaking, it was really more of a half-smile but Fran still found herself staring at him as if he had zapped her with a stun gun. Her breath hitched in her throat, her stomach gave a little flip turn and her legs—even her good one—threatened to fold beneath her.

Fran hadn't realised she had even stumbled until his hand shot out and steadied her. 'Are you OK?' he asked, frowning at her in concern.

She looked down at his long tanned fingers almost overlapping on her forearm and gave a little shiver. Her skin was a light golden honey colour from her days on the beach but nowhere near the darkness of his. Her arm was smooth and hairless while his was liberally covered with springy masculine hair, right down his arms to the backs of his hands and along each of his long fingers.

'Dr Nin?'

Fran brought her eyes back to his. 'Sorry…' She swept her tongue out over her lips. 'I'm still not all that steady on sand. It's supposed to be good physio for me…you know, walking with bare feet.'

Jacob dropped his hand from her arm, his fingers still tingling slightly even when he took the stick Rufus was poking against his thigh and threw it towards the rolling waves. 'How'd it happen?' he asked, turning back to look at her.

Something moved in her eyes, like a stagehand quickly re-arranging something on the set before the audience could notice. 'Skiing,' she said, looking away into the distance. 'In New Zealand.'

Jacob let a little silence pass.

'So, how long are you staying in town?' he asked.

'About three months or so,' she answered, trying to capture Rufus's collar as he came back with the stick. 'We should let you get on with your run.'

'I'm done,' Jacob said. 'I was going to head into the surf to cool off. Have you been in the water yet?'

'No, not yet,' she said, reaching for the dog again.

Rufus darted out of her reach and, barking madly, raced off after a seagull.

'I'll get him,' Jacob said and, putting two fingers to his mouth, gave a whistle that would have stopped a train. Rufus skidded to a halt and turned and ran back, his ears flopping and his tail wagging.

'I'll hold him while you clip on his lead,' Jacob offered.

Fran couldn't believe how uncooperative her fingers were in performing such a simple task but somehow Jacob Hawke's fingers brushing against hers as he held Rufus in place sent jolts of electricity up and down her spine. Finally the dog was back on the lead and she straightened. 'Thank you,' she said, looping the lead twice around her wrist for insurance. 'Enjoy your swim.'

She began to walk back the way she had come but Rufus proved reluctant to leave. He kept looking back at the tall figure behind, who when Fran took a covert glance was now carving his way through the surf in long easy strokes. His running shoes and socks were on the beach, along with his shorts. Fran didn't want to think too much about what he was swimming in. Male underwear was very similar to male swimwear but she didn't want to be around to make up her mind which he was wearing, if anything. She gave Rufus's lead another firm tug and headed up the path to Caro's house.

'Fran, oh, thank God you're back,' Caro said as soon as she came in the door. 'I think I need to go to hospital. I'm bleeding.'

Fran pushed aside her feelings of panic and did her best to get into doctor mode but she felt helplessly inadequate, more so because it was her sister and she couldn't summon up even a millimetre of clinical distance. 'How much blood?' she asked. 'Just a show or a steady stream?'

'A show at first and then I got a few cramps and now it's getting heavier,' Caro said, swallowing in anguish. 'I've called Nick. He's on his way.' There was the sound of a car pulling into the drive. 'Oh, thank God, that's him now.'

Fran called an ambulance first and then, after making her

sister comfortable and doing her best to reassure her brother-in-law, she quickly packed a bag for Caro to take with her to hospital.

'I won't lose the babies, will I?' Caro asked as she was loaded in the back of the ambulance a short time later, her face still white with distress.

'No, of course not, Caro—the placenta may have lifted a little, that's all. Just keep calm and relaxed and wait for a full obstetric assessment in hospital. The doctors will do everything possible to keep you all safe,' Fran said. 'Don't worry about things here. I'll look after Rufus and I'll call Mum and Dad once I know how things are going with you.'

She turned to Nick, whose face looked the colour of ash.

'Try not to panic, Nick. An early delivery is very common with twins. Caro will be much safer being monitored in hospital at this stage.' *Especially as I am practically useless at managing a sore throat, let alone something like this*, Fran thought in distress.

'Thanks, Fran,' Nick said, his throat sounding tight. 'We'll call you once we know what the go is.'

It was only after the ambulance had gone that Fran found it hard to keep from spiralling into a full-blown panic attack. She tried to keep busy, but the house seemed so empty without her sister's cheerful voice sounding out from whichever room she happened to be in.

Rufus looked downcast, his ears down, a low whining sound coming from his throat as he followed Fran about forlornly.

The telephone rang three hours later with Nick informing her he was the proud father of twin boys. Although in the neonatal unit, they were doing very well, all things considered, but would be in hospital for some weeks. There was some suggestion one of the babies might have to be trans-ferred to one of the larger teaching hospitals in Sydney for further monitoring. Nick had decided he would stay in Wollongong in a serviced apartment and had already con-tacted the education department about finding a replacement teacher. He wanted to be with Caro and the boys until they could come home as a family.

'How is Caro?' Fran asked, trying not to cry.

'She's great,' Nick said. 'She wants to speak to you. I'll hand her over.'

'Fran, you won't believe how tiny they are,' Caro gushed with maternal pride. 'I can't wait until you see them. Nick's going to send you some photos via his phone. We haven't decided on names yet. We can't quite make up our minds—silly, isn't it? We've been arguing about it for the last ten minutes. We've called Mum and Dad, they're in Italy right now, Florence, I think, or maybe it was Venice. Oh, Frannie, I'm *so* happy.'

'I'm happy for you,' Fran said, trying to ignore the tiny pang of envy that trickled through her. Caro was only two years older than her and here she was happily married with two gorgeous babies while she had nothing but a career she was too frightened to return to and no man in her life to love her the way she longed to be loved. She chided herself for being so bitter. Stuff happened in life, and it wasn't always the white picket fence and roses spilling over stuff. It was hard stuff, challenging stuff, stuff that changed everything in the rapid rise and fall of an eyelid.

When the photos of the babies came through a few minutes later, Fran allowed herself a few self-indulgent tears. She had so rarely given in to tears. Her training had toughened her up, perhaps too much, or so her mother thought, and her gruff show-no-emotion father, too, when it came to that. But now alone in a big seaside house with just a ragamuffin dog for company, Fran sobbed for her lost life, for the carefree girl she had once been and might never be again.

She didn't hear the doorbell at first, but then Rufus began to bark and scratch at the door. The doorbell was ringing continuously, as if someone was repeatedly stabbing at the button. Then someone was thumping on the door. Annoyed at the intrusion, Fran blew her nose, stuffed the tissue into her bra, and cautiously opened the heavy front door.

One of Caro and Nick's neighbours from two doors away practically fell into the hallway, his face marble white, his body shaking. 'Dr Nin? Caro told me you're a doctor. Quickly—come on, you've got to save her. My daughter…' He started to cry, great heaving sobs, each one sounding as if it was shredding his chest. 'My d-daughter, Ella, my baby fell into the pool. She's not breathing.'

Fran pushed Rufus back indoors, stepped onto the verandah and shut the door. 'Who is with your daughter now?' she asked, her heart thudding as adrenalin kicked in.

'My wife,' he said, choking back another sob. 'She's done first aid but nothing's working. You've got to help us. Please, quickly. *Come on.*'

'Have you called an ambulance?' she asked as she hurried after the distressed man into the neighbouring property, her stomach knotting with dread at what she might find.

'Yes, yes, yes, but they won't get here till it's too late. They're way out of town, on some other call. Jane thought of you. You've got to help us, please, please, *come on*!'

'It's all right…Joe, isn't it?' Fran said, recalling his name. Caro had said what a lovely family the Pelleris were, new to the town but fitting in well with everyone. Joe was a mechanic at the local service station, Jane a stay-at-home mum with three children—a toddler and two boys.

It was only a hundred metres to the Pelleris' house but Fran felt her heart rate escalating with sickening speed. A brain without oxygen couldn't survive for long. Children might last a bit longer, but even if revived, it might only be the heart and lungs that functioned. The brain could be damaged or even worse—the child might be dead. The child some parents brought into the hospital was not always the child they took home.

Every second was vital.

Every second counted.

Every second hammered at Fran's chest as she pushed through the garden gate towards the house.

Jane Pelleri was trying her best to do CPR on the baby in the family room just off the pool area, with the two little boys distressed and crying in the background.

'Jane, I'll take over now,' Fran said in a calm, doctor-in-control tone, even though her stomach was roiling with doubts and fears that she wouldn't be up to the task. This was no well-equipped A and E department. This was a family's home with baby and toddler photographs on the walls, not lifesaving resuscitation gear. Fear gripped at Fran's heart with cruel claws. What if she couldn't do this? What if she failed? Her stomach churned with nausea, her skin broke out in a sheen of perspiration and her hands shook almost uncontrollably as she tried to assess the situation.

The child was on the very springy sofa, which had made the mother's efforts at cardiac compression largely ineffective. Fran placed the infant, who looked about eighteen months old, onto her back on the carpeted floor, and tilted her head slightly back to open the airway. There seemed to be the remains of a biscuit in the child's mouth, which Fran swept out with her finger. The child was clearly not breathing and appeared cyanosed. Supporting Ella's head, Fran covered the nose and mouth with her mouth and gave five puffs, then felt for a pulse over the inner arm, then the neck.

Either there was none, or her lack of recent clinical experience was letting her down and she just wasn't sensitive enough to feel it, she thought as another pang of doubt stung her. She had to assume the child's heart had stopped. Using two fingers, Fran gently compressed the child's chest over the lower sternum, twenty rapid compressions for each couple of breaths.

Was that the right ratio? she thought in panic. It was higher in adults, lower in children and lower in infants. *Oh, God, what was the ratio?* Had her skills and training been punched out of her along with her confidence in A and E that day? Her brain became foggy with fear, dread and doubts. She couldn't do this. She was failing. She was not going to be able to save this child. How would she face the parents? What about those two little boys? Oh, God, even the photos on the walls seemed to be staring down at her in accusation. You are a failure. You are no good at this. Look at what you have done.

Fran vaguely registered a siren sounding and it seemed mere seconds before Jacob Hawke was kneeling beside her, talking to her, but it was as if it was in a vacuum. She couldn't hear him; she saw his lips moving but it was as if the sound had been muffled by her fear.

'For God's sake, Dr Nin,' Jacob bit out roughly, finally shaking her out of her stasis. 'Help me here. Keep her steady while I do the mouth-to-mouth.'

Fran blinked herself into action and held the child in position, watching in numb silence as Jacob determinedly worked at the breaths and compressions for what seemed like hours, made worse by the howling boys and now hysterical mother. Had the child's colour improved, or was it Fran's imagination?

Unexpectedly, the infant coughed, then seemed to convulse. She vomited up some water, coughed again, and then started wailing, the colour of her face turning from lavender to cherry red.

In the distance another wailing sound could be heard, this one the reassuring whine of the ambulance approaching at speed.

'Mummy-y!' the toddler croaked over another cough.

'Keep her on her side,' Jacob directed the child's mother. 'She'll be fine but she needs to go to hospital for a proper check of her airways and lungs.'

Fran sat back on her heels, her breathing hurting her chest as cautious relief flooded through her. Ella was alive. Ella was breathing. Ella was alive...

Jacob met her eyes, something in his ice-cold gaze ripping through her like shards of ice. 'Everything all right, Dr Nin?' he asked in a tone as arctic as his eyes.

'F-fine,' she said, using a nearby chair to pull herself to her feet. 'I...I lost concentration for a moment...that was all.'

'Yeah, well, it only takes a moment and it's too late,' he muttered in an undertone, well out of hearing of the distressed family.

Fran wanted to be angry at him but her nerves were still shredded. She felt as if her whole body was hanging in pieces, none of them connected to each other. She could barely get her legs to move. Her head was spinning so much she thought she might be sick, but somehow she pulled herself together for the family's sake.

'I don't know how to thank you,' Jane was still sobbing as

she cradled her daughter. 'I don't know how she got out to the pool. The gate was closed, I'm sure it was. I'm always so careful.'

'It's hard to watch kids all the time,' Fran said, glancing at the two boys who were still looking shocked, huddled together in the corner of the room.

Once the ambulance officers arrived Fran filled them in with what had happened. The officers were not trained paramedics, just volunteers, but the older man called Jack seemed very competent and experienced as he handled the little patient.

Within a few minutes, both mother and child were in the back of the ambulance, heading for Wollongong Hospital for proper assessment and observation of Ella.

Another police car pulled into the driveway almost as soon as the ambulance had pulled out, and Joe gave Fran a worried look. 'What are more cops doing here?' he asked, placing an arm around each of his boys.

'It's pretty standard procedure in cases like this,' Fran said, although personally she questioned the timing of it. The traumatised father and his young sons were obviously desperate to get in the car and follow the ambulance to hospital, but she understood from other cases she had dealt with the importance of ruling out any suspicious circumstances.

Jacob went over to the police vehicle and spoke to the officer on duty. The car backed out of the driveway a few moments later and Jacob came back up the path to where Joe and his boys were waiting with Fran.

Jacob exchanged a brief unreadable glance with Fran before he reached for Joe's hand. 'I'm sorry I didn't get a chance to introduce myself earlier. I'm Sergeant Jacob Hawke.' He smiled down at the boys. 'Hi, guys.' He bent down to their level. 'What are your names?'

'I—I'm Joey and he's Romeo,' the older of the boys said.

'Those are great names—Italian, right?' Jacob asked, glancing at the father for verification.

Joe nodded, his throat rising and falling over a tight swallow. 'Sergeant, I think it would be best if we talk in private. I don't want the boys to be upset any further.'

Fran stepped forward. 'I'd be happy to fix the boys a juice or something,' she said, and turned to them.

'How about it, Romeo and Joey? Can you show me where Mummy keeps everything?'

The little boys led the way to the kitchen where Fran poured them both orange juice and gave them two chocolate-chip cookies apiece. After a while their dark brown eyes began to lose their haunted, hollow look and they even started to chat about their favourite toys and games.

After half an hour the boys' father came in, followed by Jacob. 'Thank you again, Dr Nin, and you too, Sergeant,' Joe said. 'I know Jane already thanked you both but you really did save our little girl today. If there's anything, and I mean *anything*, we can ever do for you, just let me know. It goes without saying you won't be charged a cent if you need your car serviced at my workshop, Dr Nin. Just book it in any time.'

'Thank you, Joe,' Fran said, feeling every type of fraud. She hadn't saved Ella, that had been Jacob, and both of them knew it. The family had been too upset to notice and had just assumed as she was a doctor that she was responsible for the miracle of bringing their precious daughter back to them. 'That's very kind of you but I was only doing my…er…' she flushed and hated herself for it '…what I've been trained to do.'

'We should let you get on your way to the hospital to be with your wife and daughter,' Jacob said to Joe, and then, turning to face Fran, asked, 'Would you like a lift back to your sister's house?'

Fran considered refusing but her leg was still throbbing from her hundred-metre dash earlier, and she was also concerned about how long Rufus had been locked in the laundry back at the house. 'Thank you,' she said, brushing her hair back with her hand. 'That would be great.'

After saying farewell to the Pelleri boys and their father, Jacob led the way out to the police vehicle, opening the passenger door for her and standing patiently as she eased into the seat.

He waited until they were on their way before he spoke. 'When was the last time you performed resuscitation on a child?'

Fran stiffened in her seat. 'Look, it was tough in there, OK? The family was hysterical and there was no resus gear at hand. I'm not used to working at the coalface like that. I've been in a high-tech city teaching hospital all my working life.'

Her words hung in the ensuing silence, each one of them making her feel even more disgusted with her incompetence under pressure. She of all people should have been able to handle an emergency, no matter what equipment was at hand. She could just imagine what Jacob was thinking: she was a stuck-up city slicker who couldn't stop a nosebleed without a trauma team on hand for back-up. He was very probably right, Fran thought with another wave of disgust at herself.

'It could so easily have gone the other way but it didn't,' Jacob said after a moment. 'Small communities like this don't cope well with tragedy. It affects everyone.'

Fran bit her lip as those terrified little boys' faces drifted into her consciousness. 'Yes…I know…'

Jacob glanced across at her. 'It seems one of the boys left the gate unlocked. The mother turned her back for a minute, the father was occupied elsewhere and suddenly the family was a minute or two from tragedy.'

Fran looked at him, her forehead creasing. 'That's not going to be made public, is it? About one of the boys leaving the gate unlocked?'

He drew in a breath as he turned into the Atkinses' driveway. 'As you are probably aware, whenever there is a case of drowning or near-drowning the police are required to attend and submit a media report in the interests of public education to make the community safer for children. So many parents are unaware of the dangers of leaving children unsupervised or the laws regarding adequate fencing around pools.'

Fran felt her body tensing. 'You didn't answer my question,' she said. 'Joey is only six years old, Romeo only four. It would be morally reprehensible to name and shame either one of them for something that was just an unfortunate accident.'

He killed the engine and turned to look at her. 'I am confident the incident was not a result of parental neglect or insufficient supervision. When Joe and I inspected the catch on the gate we found it to be faulty. It sometimes locks, it sometimes doesn't. If it is anyone's fault, it is the manufacturer's. The Pelleris have only been in Pelican Bay a few months. The pool and the fence surrounding it were only installed a couple of weeks ago.'

Fran felt her shoulders come down in relief. 'I'm sorry,' she said. 'I didn't mean to bite your head off but those little boys...well, it would destroy their childhood to be blamed for something like that.'

'Speaking of little boys,' he said as he unclipped his seat

belt, 'how is your sister? I heard she was rushed to hospital earlier today and gave birth to twins.'

'She's doing really well, although the babies have to stay in the neonatal unit for a while,' Fran said. 'I'm not sure what their names are yet. That was still under discussion last time I spoke to her.'

'That's great news,' he said. 'They'll make wonderful parents. They seem a nice couple.'

'They are,' she said. 'Nick is a lovely man. My sister is very happy.'

There was a small silence.

'So…how about you?' he asked.

Fran felt her fingers tighten in her lap. 'What about me?'

His light blue gaze bored into hers. 'Are you currently involved with someone? A boyfriend, fiancé, husband?'

She looked at him, conscious of her face heating under his scrutiny. 'I'm not sure why you're asking me such personal questions. Tell me something, Sergeant, does every newcomer to town suffer the same interrogation from you?'

His lips twitched but it still couldn't be called a smile. 'Not the dating sort, huh?'

She pulled her mouth tight. 'Actually, I am not the sort of person to talk about personal details with complete strangers,' she clipped back.

She shoved open the passenger door, throwing him an icy look over one shoulder. 'Thank you for the lift.'

His mouth took on that mocking slant that annoyed her so much. 'I take it someone like me broke your heart.'

'Actually, he was nothing like you,' Fran said. 'And he didn't break my heart. He was—' She stopped, suddenly re-alising how cleverly he had manipulated her into revealing far more than she wanted to reveal.

'He was…?' he prompted with a hook of one brow.

She clamped her lips together and swung her legs out of the car, but the weakness in her left leg made her stumble.

Jacob tried to reach her from inside the car but she pitched forward and landed heavily on the gravel driveway. He bit back a stiff curse and leapt out to go to her aid.

'Are you OK?' he asked, helping her to her feet.

She tried to brush him off, but he could see the pain like a misty shadow in her grey-blue eyes, so he kept his hold gentle but firm as she regained her balance.

He ran his gaze over her. 'Your knees are bleeding,' he said. 'Let me help you inside to clean them up.'

'I'm all right,' she said, but it was clear she wasn't. She looked shaken and pale and her bottom lip was trembling slightly, as if she was fighting tears. It had been tough at the Pelleris', he was the first to admit that, but she was a qualified medic, for pity's sake. If she was going to last any time in the bush she would have to toughen up, and fast.

Jacob put an arm around her shoulders and helped her to the front door, his body springing to awareness of her petite feminine frame tucked into the strength of his. Her long blonde hair tickled the bare skin on his arm, and he could smell its alluring summer fragrance of frangipani and coconut.

After his break-up with Melissa he had been determined not to do the rebound thing, but weeks and then months had gone by and he had started to forget how nice it felt to hold someone close. However, Dr Frances Nin was just the sort of woman he usually avoided. Touchy, argumentative and prickly, not exactly the qualities he was looking for in a life partner. But he had to admit she packed quite a visual punch.

Rufus barked as they came in but Jacob issued him with a

stern command to sit in case he bumped against Fran. 'Which way to the first-aid kit?' he asked.

'Look, Sergeant Hawke,' she began, 'this is totally unnecessary. It's just a scratch.'

'Jacob.'

She blinked at him. 'Sorry?'

'You can call me Jacob,' he said with a crooked tilt of his lips. 'Pelican Bay isn't big on formality, or hasn't anyone told you that?'

'Jacob…' She slipped out of his hold, her cheeks the colour of a soft pink rose. 'Thanks for the lift but really I would much rather be alone right now.'

Jacob made an L with his fingers and rested it against his chin and mouth as he looked down at her musingly.

'He really did a good job on you, didn't he?'

Her chin came up and a storm brewed in her grey-blue eyes. 'I have already told you I am not interested in discussing my private life,' she said.

'What was his name?'

Her hands fisted by her sides, flashes of anger in her gaze as it clashed with his. 'I realise it is a part of your job to ask questions but to put it bluntly, Sergeant Hawke, I have no intention of answering them.'

'Where's the first-aid kit?' he asked again.

She crossed her arms and angled her head towards the door. 'I have two words for you, Sergeant. Leave. Now.'

Jacob moved past her to where he supposed the nearest bathroom was, a part of him enjoying the verbal tussle with her. He liked the way her eyes lost their soulless look when she battled head to head with him. He suspected behind that fragile the-world-is-against-me demeanour was a spirited young woman who just needed some time to sort herself out.

'What do you think you're doing?' she asked as she limped after him into the downstairs bathroom.

He opened a couple of drawers below the basin before he found what he was looking for. 'Sit on the toilet seat while I clean those scratches,' he said.

She stood mulishly, still glaring at him with those thundercloud eyes. 'I am quite capable of seeing to my own scratches, Sergeant Hawke. I am a doctor, remember?'

He dabbed a cotton-wool ball with antiseptic. 'I'm glad to hear you say that,' he said. 'When word gets around about your heroic success in saving Ella Pelleri, just about every resident in Pelican Bay is going to be knocking on your door for a consultation.'

'We both know it wasn't me that saved her,' she said.

His eyes locked on hers before he returned to assembling the first-aid items on the bench. 'I figure it's like loosening the lid on a jar for someone.'

'What?'

He looked sideways to see her frowning at him in confusion. 'When I was a little kid…' He paused for a second before continuing, 'My mother had trouble unscrewing jars, or so she said. I would try my hardest to unscrew it but in the end I would hand it back to her, but each and every time she would say I had loosened it for her. The way I see it, you had the situation more or less in control, apart from momentary panic, which could have happened to anyone given the circumstances. I just loosened the lid on it for you.'

Her mouth pulled even tighter but he saw a flicker of consternation pass through her eyes. 'Even so, I'm not obliged to see anyone while I am here in town,' she said. 'I haven't even got a prescription pad with me.'

He placed a hand on her shoulder and with gentle pressure

forced her to sit on the closed toilet seat. 'I am sure there are prescription pads at the clinic as well as anything else needed to run a small one-doctor practice.'

Fran felt her breathing go out of whack as he hunkered down in front of her. He was wearing his gunbelt complete with handcuffs and mobile phone and radio, adding to his dangerous, don't-mess-with-me air. Her shoulder was still tingling from the pressure of his large warm hand, the nerves beneath her skin tap-dancing in delight. She couldn't help staring at his hands. His fingers were twice the thickness of hers, long and tanned with neatly clipped square nails. The knuckles of his right hand were grazed, and she wondered if he had got that in the line of duty or doing some sort of handyman job.

'Ouch!' She jerked back as he dabbed her scraped knees with the cotton wool.

'Sorry, but, believe me, this is hurting me more than it's hurting you.'

Fran peered at him through narrowed eyes. 'Are you laughing at me, Sergeant Hawke?' she asked.

He gave her a glinting half-smile that did strange things to her stomach, making it tip upside down like a quickly flipped pancake. 'Now, why would I do that, Dr Nin?' he asked.

She scowled as he continued to dab at her knees. 'I wish you would stop calling me that.'

He met her gaze in between dabs. 'Too formal for you?'

She blew out a sigh. 'I don't feel like a doctor any more… at least I don't want to.'

He placed two pieces of sticky plaster on each knee before he straightened. 'So you're going to throw away all those years of study to do what? Go on endless holidays?' he asked, a disapproving frown narrowing the distance between his eyes as he looked down at her.

Fran stood up gingerly, conscious of how close he was standing to her. She could smell his male smell, warmth, a hint of citrus and a hint of perspiration full of sexy male pheromones, which was dangerously attractive. 'I don't know,' she said in a deliberately airy tone. 'I'm still thinking about it.'

He scrunched up the wrappers and tossed them in the pedal bin near his feet. 'Well, while you're thinking about it, why not think about this?' he said, locking his gaze with hers. 'There are people living here who need a doctor, not next week, not next month, but today. You don't have to put in a ninety-hour week—no one is asking you to. But why not just a couple of hours, once or twice a week until a replacement is found?'

Fran would have pushed past him but it would have meant touching him and that she wanted to avoid. She'd had enough trouble keeping her head while he'd been tending to her knees. Feeling his gentle touch had switched on sensations she could still feel charging through her body. She lowered her gaze and ran her tongue over her lips, feeling cornered and confused. 'I'm not interested, Sergeant Hawke,' she said with as much firmness as she could muster, which wasn't much.

Something about him made her feel deeply disturbed. It wasn't just his male presence—it was also his commanding air of authority. He was a man used to getting his own way. She could see it in the carved-from-stone contours of his jaw, not to mention the ice-hard focus of his gaze when it locked on hers.

The phone on his belt began to ring and Fran let out a sigh of relief as he moved past her to answer it. Her reprieve was brief, however, for in less than thirty seconds Jacob was back, his car keys already tinkling in his hand.

'There's been an accident out on Valley Road,' he said. 'A teenager has fallen off her horse—sounds like at the very least a broken leg. The ambulance is away, taking Ella Pelleri to Wollongong Hospital, so the clinic receptionist has called in Careflight. We'll drop by the ambulance station and pick up their trauma bag. You can stabilise the victim until the chopper arrives.'

'But I—' Fran quickly bit back her protest. What would be the point in saying she couldn't handle it, that two emergencies in one day was asking way too much of her? She could see from the look in Jacob's eyes there was no way he was going to take no for an answer.

CHAPTER THREE

WITH the police siren screeching, Jacob hit speeds Fran had only seen at her Formula One medical training days in Melbourne a couple of years ago. Thankfully the breakneck pace took her mind off everything but surviving the journey in one piece. Even though he had supposedly only been in town only a few months, he seemed to know his way around the back roads, she thought as they arrived at a large property with white post-and-rail fences in less than ten minutes, notwithstanding their detour to the ambulance station for the trauma kit.

Jacob pulled up in the main driveway and grabbed the trauma kit from the back seat while Fran got out on legs that were still smarting from their tumble on the gravel earlier.

In the middle of the main paddock in front of a colonial cottage there was a small group of people—mostly men, from what Fran could see—surrounding a teenage girl lying in the dust. A horse was some distance off, lying on its side, its chest and belly rising and falling as if every breath was like trying to lift a road train off its chest.

The gate to the paddock was at least two hundred metres away, so there was little choice but to climb over the fence.

The oldest of the men broke away from the group and ran across the field towards them. Jacob helped Fran over the fence, and then handed over the trauma kit before scaling the fence effortlessly himself.

'Candi's broken her leg, Sergeant Hawke,' Jim Broderick, the girl's father, said, looking pinched about his weather beaten face. 'We've done what we can to make her comfortable but she's in a helluva lot of pain.'

'G'day, Jim. This is Dr Nin, Carolyn Atkins's sister, visiting from Melbourne,' Jacob said as they made their way to the injured girl. 'She's very kindly offered to help out until the Careflight arrives.'

'Thank God,' Jim said, relief relaxing his tight features for a moment. 'I've been nearly out of my mind since I heard there was no ambulance for at least a couple of hours. My poor kid's in agony.'

Fran could see the girl's right thigh was bent back at a right angle. Thankfully her riding boot and sock had been removed, although her foot was obviously blue. She was rigid with severe pain, her teeth chattering and tears streaming amidst the dust on her young freckled face. At least the girl was conscious which made Fran's panic ease a little. She worked hard on remaining focussed, keeping her head as clear as she could so Jacob would see she was not completely useless in a crisis.

'Candi, we've got a doctor here to help you,' Jacob said soothingly as he put the bag down for Fran to access. 'A helicopter is coming soon to take you to hospital.'

'Hi, Candi, my name is Fran,' Fran said as she opened the trauma kit. 'It looks like you've got a nasty leg injury. I can see you're being very brave but let's see if we can do something about the pain, shall we?'

The girl nodded, fresh tears rolling down her cheeks. 'Is Cheeky all right?' she asked, trying to twist her head to see where she thought her horse was.

Jacob exchanged a quick glance with Fran, his eyes communicating much more than words. Fran caught a glimpse of Jim Broderick's grim expression and turned back to Candi. 'You're the one we are concentrating on now, Candi,' she said as she gloved up and drew 10 mg of morphine and 10 mg of diazepam into a syringe. Inserting a canula into Candi's left arm, she administered the drugs and attached a litre of saline, instructing Jacob to pump it in through the IV pump set she had attached.

'We're going to have to straighten the leg to try to regain the blood supply to your foot,' Fran said. 'I'm sorry, Candi, this will hurt but I've given you some pain relief, which should be taking effect now, and we really have to straighten out your leg to avoid permanent damage.'

Under Fran's direction Jim put his arms around his daughter's chest while Jacob helped to stabilise her position. Fran gently pulled and rotated Candi's leg to the normal anatomical position, accompanied by a scream of pain from the girl.

Fran felt for the dorsalis pedis pulse, which had reassuringly returned, together with a pink colour of the foot. She then took a blow-up splint from the kit, applied it to the leg and was about to show Jacob where to blow into the valve to inflate it but he was already onto it.

'You did really well, Candi,' Fran said, resting back on her heels in the dust of the paddock. 'Your leg's going to be fine. You'll have to have a cast, of course, and no riding for a couple of months at the very least.'

Candi's eyes were a little glazed from the drugs she had

been given but she still seemed determined to see where her horse was. 'Let me up,' she said, struggling to lift herself up on her elbows. 'I want to see Cheeky.'

'I'm sorry, love,' Jim said, holding her back down. 'There's nothing we can do.'

Fran watched as the young girl's face crumpled, the pain of her leg quite obviously nothing to what she was going through now.

'Don't shoot him!' Candi cried, still trying to get out of her father's hold, her flailing hands totally ineffectual other than to stir up more dust over everybody. 'Don't you dare shoot him!'

Fran felt her chest go tight as she glanced to where the horse was vainly trying to lift its head, its big, lustrous eyes wild with pain and fear. She wondered if the animal somehow knew what was going to happen to him, that this was the end of the road. Fran had seen that look in terminally ill patients' eyes before. The light of hope fading as realisation dawned. There was no going back, no miracles to pull out of the box.

The sound of the helicopter arriving didn't quite deaden the sound of the rifle, but thankfully the increase in pain relief Fran had quickly administered meant that Candi hadn't heard either sound.

'I don't know how to thank you,' Jim said to Fran as his daughter was being loaded onto the aircraft. 'My wife passed away two years ago. Like Sergeant Hawke's mother, she had breast cancer. When she died last week it brought back all my memories. And now this... Candi's all I've got.' He gave another tight swallow.

'If anything happened to her...'

Fran touched him on the arm, her throat so tight she could barely speak. *Jacob's mother had died just a week or so ago?*

Her brain tumbled with the information, like clothes all twisted and knotted in an overloaded dryer. He had said nothing. Not a word. But, then, it wasn't as if she knew him well enough to exchange anything but the most basic of information. But had he told anyone? If Jim Broderick knew, surely Beryl at the store would have known also. Fran could sense Jacob was a very private sort of person, but still…

Somehow she brought herself back to the moment to concentrate on Candi's worried father. 'Candi will be fine, Mr Broderick. She's a very brave girl. You must be very proud of her.'

'I am,' he said. 'She'll be back in the saddle for sure. Once that cast is off, you just watch her. I just know she'll be back.'

Fran stood a few minutes later by Jacob's side as the chopper lifted off with both Candi and Jim Broderick on board.

'I didn't realise your mother had died so recently,' she said, looking up at him. 'I'm very sorry for your loss.'

Fran was conscious of her words—her totally inadequate words—hanging in the dry, dusty air for a long moment.

'Thank you.' His eyes moved away from hers. 'But it wasn't sudden and she was well prepared for it.'

And what about you? Fran wanted to ask. *Were you prepared for it?* But before she could get the words out he broke the small silence.

'You did a great job, Dr Nin. You handled Candi's injuries well under the circumstances.'

Fran looked back at the scene of the accident. 'Did they have to shoot the horse when she expressly asked them not to?' she asked, looking up at Jacob with a frown pulling at her brow. 'Why couldn't they call a vet or something? Surely it would have been a bit more humane.'

He dusted off his trousers where the dust had clung to his knees. 'This is the country, Dr Nin,' he said in a pragmatic tone. 'The nearest vet is two and a half hours away. Just like doctors and police, vets are hard to attract and keep in places like this. The community is small, so making a living for a professional is harder than in the city. We have to do what we can with what we have. Sometimes that means that animals get shot rather than another form of euthanasia, and patients go for days or weeks without medical care.'

Fran pursed her mouth as she inspected his unreadable expression for a beat or two. 'Are you lecturing me, Sergeant Hawke?'

He hooked his thumbs into his gunbelt as his eyes met hers. 'You've got the skills; this place has the need of those skills, and you're here for a couple of months. You work it out.'

She bit down on her bottom lip. 'You don't know what you're asking…'

Jacob led the way back to the police vehicle, this time via the gate rather than have her scramble in an ungainly manner over the fence. 'Jim talked about his daughter getting back in the saddle,' he said as held the gate open for her. 'I would imagine, given what she's just gone through, that will be a huge challenge. Different horse, maybe a different saddle, but the same skills apply.'

Fran frowned as she went through the gate. Was he somehow referring to her situation? Surely Caro hadn't told him? She had made her sister promise. No one was to know. Fran wanted to allow herself time to come to terms with what had happened without having to go over it again and again every time someone new met her. Anyway, Jacob had implied he'd only met Caro and Nick once or twice. Surely Caro wouldn't have had time to engineer any of her matchmaking tricks. Or had she?

Fran narrowed her gaze as she sent a covert glance Jacob's way, but his expression was shadowed by his police hat, making it impossible for her to read it.

'How are your knees feeling?' he asked once they were back in the police vehicle.

'To borrow your own words, Sergeant Hawke, you did a good job.'

He gave her one of his fleeting smiles. 'You really like to keep your professional distance, don't you?'

Fran arched her brows at him. 'You're the one who keeps calling me Dr Nin when I've told you I don't want to be called that.'

'You don't like your name?' he asked. 'I admit it's a bit unusual. But it kind of suits you. Short and to the point.'

'It's actually French,' Fran said, deciding to overlook his provocative comment in case it led to another showdown. 'Apparently amongst the twigs of my family tree I am related to the writer Anais Nin.'

'That's quite a name drop,' he said, darting a quick glance her way as he turned the vehicle towards town.

'My mother used to read her stuff. She said it was highly sensual, or words to that effect.'

Fran examined his features during a small silence. 'I really am very sorry about your mother,' she said softly. 'It must still seem unreal to you.'

He sent another quick, unreadable glance her way. 'No, actually, it's me who should be apologising,' he said, his tone sounding gruff. 'I got the phone call from the hospital the day we had that near collision. I was rushing to get back to the station to sign off some paperwork needed for a court case before I drove to Sydney to organise the funeral.'

Fran mentally cringed at how she had shouted at him on

the roadside and then stormed into the station, not for a moment realising what he had been going through. She had come across as a ranting virago, intent on lecturing him when he had just received the most devastating of news. 'I'm so sorry,' she said again. 'Had she been ill for long?'

'Yeah.' He turned out of Valley Road into the one that led past the bay. 'She was diagnosed a couple of years after my father was killed. It took eighteen years to kill her but she put up a very brave fight.'

'You were close to her?'

This time his glance had a small rueful smile attached. 'I wasn't exactly a mummy's boy or anything but I loved her and I will miss her. She was a good woman, brave and strong even though life had thrown her some rough stuff.'

Fran felt herself sink even further into the passenger seat. She felt like a complete coward, baulking at the first hurdle that had come along, instead of working her way through her fears to find her rightful place back in the world.

But the thought of going back…

'I would have liked to have been with her when she died,' Jacob added. 'But without a doctor in town it wasn't possible. She needed strong pain relief and a few weeks ago decided to go back to Sydney. I brought her down most weekends if I wasn't on duty. She loved the beach. She used to sit for hours on the deck and watch the waves rolling in.'

Fran was starting to see why he thought her refusal to perform as a part-time doctor in the Bay seemed so selfish and shallow. No wonder he was on her back all the time, trying to bully her into a job she felt unable to perform with any competency. She considered telling him but then swiftly changed her mind. He might feel compelled to take her on as some sort of project, just as some of her colleagues had tried to do.

'I'm so sorry things didn't work out for her or for you,' she said, drawing in a scratchy sigh as she looked at the sparkling waters of the bay as it came into view.

The waves were rolling in evenly now, the fringe of white sand against the turquoise water picture-postcard perfect.

If only her life was as perfect, but, then, whose life ever was? Even the happiest and most successful people eventually had to face some sort of tragedy during the course of their lives. The Pelleris very nearly had, and the Brodericks, although saved from disaster this time, had not been so lucky in the past. And then there was Jacob and his mother…

After a moment she turned back to look at him. 'You said your father was killed. How did he die?'

His face changed, his mouth becoming a flat line of tension, his jaw with its shadow of dark stubble locking like a padlock. 'He was shot.'

The three words hung in the air.

Bang. Bang. Bang.

Fran pressed her lips together as she let the silence ring with the echo of his gunfire statement.

'Was it…?' She searched for the right words, even though she knew deep down there were none. 'Was it an accident?'

The look he gave her was bitter, angry. 'He was murdered,' he said, 'in cold blood.'

She was barely conscious of the way her hands were twisting into knots. 'What happened?' she asked in one of those crime-show-character whispers that usually irritated her so much.

'My father owned a service station—like Joe Pelleri's here in the Bay,' Jacob said. 'It was a family affair. Mum did the bookwork; I worked there after school and Saturdays.'

'You don't have siblings?' Fran asked.

He shook his head. 'Nope. There was just me. Mum had a bit of trouble in that department. She'd had about three, it might have even been four, miscarriages before me. Once I arrived safely she decided to quit while she was ahead.'

Fran let the silence stretch, waiting for him to fill it.

He took his time about it. He drove all the way to her sister's house, parked in the drive and switched off the engine before he turned in his seat to look at her. 'I'm probably keeping you from something important.'

'No,' she said. 'You're not. Please…why don't you come in and have a coffee or something? It's been a long day and I think I owe you some sort of apology for how I bawled you out the other day. If only I had known…'

'A coffee sounds great,' he said, surprising her. Fran had somehow thought he would want to hightail it out of her presence, especially since he had let his guard down, which she suspected he rarely did.

He suited his name. Those piercing blue intelligent eyes of his reminded her of a bird of prey, looking down as he rode the thermal currents that elevated him above the rest of the world, patiently assessing when it was time to strike.

Fran was conscious of how dusty and dirty she was as she led him into the house, conscious too of how his presence behind her made her limp seem more of a disfigurement than normal. One of the first things she had noticed about him had been his long, strong legs, the way they'd strode across the ground with purpose, the way they'd hugged his powerful motorbike, the way he'd stood without a hint of a wobble in his stance.

'Do you mind if I take a minute to freshen up?' she asked, hoping she wasn't blushing as much as she felt she was.

'No problem,' he said, bending down to scratch Rufus's ears. He had bounded up to greet him with his ebullient personality on show. 'This boy here looks like he needs a run. I'll be back in ten.'

'Right…' Fran said, wondering why her heart was playing leapfrog as she watched him leave the house, with Rufus bounding excitedly at his side.

'Stop it,' she said in an undertone, turning towards the bathroom. 'Stop it right now. You're not yourself right now. You don't even know what you want to do with your life, much less who you want to spend it with. Just stop it.'

Jacob didn't need to find a ball to throw. Rufus did that part for him, coming up to him with it in his smiling mouth, his plumy tail slashing from side to side in glee. Jacob grimaced as he took the slimy and ragged tennis ball from the dog's mouth, and then threw it as far as he could, watching as the mutt bounded off, ears flapping as the ball rolled down the embankment into the wild part of the garden.

The sun was still warm and another storm seemed to be brewing. He could feel the tension in the air, or maybe he was kidding himself. Maybe it was the tension he could feel in his body every time he was near the little pint-sized blonde doctor who didn't want to be a doctor any more. Apart from the near disaster at the Pelleris', Fran had handled Candi's emergency with the sort of calm competence this town needed. She was exactly what Pelican Bay needed. Hell, maybe she was exactly what *he* needed right now.

But did he really want to get entangled with a woman who was prepared to throw away her career on a whim? As far as he was concerned, a broken leg sustained while on a skiing holiday was no excuse for walking away from a profession that was in such demand these days. A huge amount of public money had been invested in her education, and for her to walk away from it seemed almost criminal. But maybe she was one of those shallow types, a member of Generation X or Y or whatever it was called these days, who wanted to flit from place to place on a permanent holiday, not unlike his ex, Melissa. He didn't know much about Fran's background but he could see there was no shortage of money. She drove a top-end car with all the safety features, and her clothes were high-street fashion—and she wore them well, he had to admit. She wore a bikini and a sarong even better. He could still see her sexy figure in that filmy shroud—the image was burned at the back of his eyeballs. Every day since, he had dreamed of peeling it off her to reveal what was underneath.

Rufus came back with the ball in his mouth, his tail wagging proudly.

'You want me to throw this again?' Jacob asked.

Rufus dropped the ball and, wriggling his back end, barked in reply.

Jacob smiled and, bending down, picked up the saliva-sodden ball and threw it down the pathway to the beach. 'Go get it, boy,' he said, and then, taking his own advice, turned and went back to the house.

Fran looked at herself in the mirror and grimaced. A quick shower had removed the dust and grime but it had done nothing about the shadows under her eyes. Her hair was in limp strands over her back and shoulders, but it would take at least twenty minutes to dry it.

Hmm… Twenty minutes with a hand-held hairdryer when she could be spending the same time with the best-looking man she had seen since…well since for ever. Anton Leeton, her ex-part-time boyfriend, was no billboard model but he was certainly no reason to reach for the soothing eyedrops either.

In the end Fran came out dressed in one of her sister's sundresses. That was one of the best things about having a sister, especially a recently pregnant one who had a whole wardrobe of designer clothes that were currently useless.

Jacob turned to face her as she came in, his eyes sweeping over her in a blood-heating manner. 'Wow, that was a quick change,' he said. 'I can't promise the same transformation but if I could at least remove your sister's dog's saliva from my hands I might be able to turn myself into presentable company.'

Fran's lips flickered with a smile as she waved an arm towards the bathroom. 'It's all yours,' she said. 'I'll put some coffee on.'

'Sounds great.'

While the coffee was brewing Fran took the cake she had baked for her sister…had it only been the day before? It seemed like so much had happened in the short time since she had creamed the butter and sugar and carefully folded in the flour.

Her sister was now a mother, a young toddler's life had been saved and a young teenager was now on her way to hospital with a leg that would mend a whole lot sooner than her heart, if she was any judge.

Jacob came out just as she was placing the pink iced coconut cake on a pretty flowery plate she had given Caro for her thirtieth birthday.

'Mmm, that coffee smells good,' he said. 'And is that cake home baked?'

'Sure is,' Fran said, pushing a cup and plate across the island bench towards him. 'My mother is a hospitality teacher at high school. She was pretty adamant Carolyn and I learn how to cook from a young age. I used to hate it when I was forced to do it, but now I'm glad she persisted with it. I find baking relaxing, although it's no fun baking for just one person.'

His eyes met hers across the bench. 'So when you're not skiing in New Zealand or visiting your sister, you live alone?'

Fran snagged her lip with her teeth and concentrated on stirring her coffee, which, because she didn't take sugar or milk was rather a superfluous thing to do. She wondered if he would notice. Cops were pretty good at that sort of thing. 'Yes,' she said, putting down the teaspoon with a little ping on the bench. 'I live alone.'

'You're right about the cooking-for-one-person thing,' he said, raising his cup to his lips and taking a sip.

Fran cradled her cup in her hands as she looked at him. How could a man look so sexy just drinking coffee? she wondered. In fact, how could a man look so damned sexy in a police uniform that in spite of his quick clean-up was still dusty and a little crumpled?

'Oh?' she said, trying to keep track of the conversation while her mind was conjuring up images of him without his uniform, like the day she had seen him on the beach, tanned and glistening, those long, strong muscular legs powering through the sand…

'Yeah,' he said, putting his cup down to take the slice of cake she'd placed on a plate for him. 'I've been on my own now for five months and three days. Don't know the hours but that's close enough.'

'Is that the sound of a heart that hasn't quite mended?' Fran asked.

He gave her a twisted smile. 'No, that's the sound of a man who is relieved he doesn't have to answer to someone day in day out. I lock people up all the time, Dr Nin. Call it hypocritical of me but I don't like it when someone does it to me.'

'Your…er…wife was the possessive type?'

'Melissa and I were dating, not married. That was my choice, not hers. She wanted the whole shebang, the big society wedding, the two-point-one kids and the nine-to-five husband.'

He paused for a beat or two before he went on, 'I'm a cop. There's no such thing as nine-to-five criminals, or for that matter nine-to-five emergencies. Even if I took a desk job there would be times when duty would have to take priority. And in any case, I wanted to spend some time on the coast with my mother. That was the hammer that drove the last nail in the coffin of our relationship. Melissa didn't want to share me with a dying woman and I refused to compromise.'

Fran took a sip of her coffee and wondered if his casual I'm-over-it attitude was covering deeper hurt. Men were often hard to read emotionally. Showing vulnerability was a no-no, particularly in Australian men, and particularly in cops.

'So you live on your own here at Pelican Bay?' she asked.

'Yes, in a house further down the beach from here,' he said. 'It's pretty secluded. You can see it from the rock pools if you know what you're looking for. It's on the top of the cliff.'

'You must have great views.'

The corner of his mouth twitched slightly. 'Sometimes the view is better than others.'

Fran dropped her gaze, wondering if he had seen her on the beach more than once. She had often taken a book down and sat under the spindly sheoak trees near the rock pools. Once, only a couple of days ago, she had taken her bikini top off so she could feel the sun warming her naked flesh. Caro had assured her it was totally private, that hardly anyone came along and if they did you could see them for miles and had time to cover up.

'Nice cake,' Jacob said, brushing some crumbs onto his plate.

'Thank you,' Fran said, feeling a blush steal over her cheeks. God, she was so pathetic, clutching at the slightest compliment as if it might be the last she'd ever get. 'Um…would you like another slice?'

'No, thanks, but another coffee would be good.'

She poured him another cup and passed him the milk and sugar, watching as he spooned in two and a half teaspoons and a generous dash of milk.

'You didn't finish telling me what happened to your father,' she said.

His expression clouded as it had in the car earlier and she noticed his grip on his coffee mug tightened. 'It was an armed robbery,' he said, putting his mug on the bench as if he was afraid he was going to snap its handle. 'My father was on his own that evening. Two men came in and one cleaned out the till and the other shot my father. He would have lived but by the time help arrived it was too late to save him.'

Fran felt a shudder of horror go through her. 'I'm so sorry. How dreadful for you and your poor mother to lose him that way.'

'Yeah,' he said, picking up his cup and looking at the contents for a moment. 'It was.'

'Is that why you became a police officer?' she asked.

'One of the reasons,' he said, and then after a small silence asked, 'Have you given any thought to my suggestion?'

'What suggestion was that?' Fran asked, even though she knew and had been silently dreading this conversation ever since they had left Candi Broderick and her father with the Careflight crew.

'Filling in at the clinic for an hour or two,' he said, holding her gaze with magnetic force.

Fran finally dragged her gaze away and toyed with the barely touched cake on her plate, squishing a crumb beneath the pad of her index finger as if it was a tiny ant. 'It's not that simple, Sergeant...'

He didn't speak, which she knew was a clever tactic to keep her talking. She'd seen enough crime shows to know how it worked. She would start out determined to keep her mouth closed, but the silence would grow teeth that would gnaw at her until she began to fidget. And he would stand there, like he was doing now, his arms folded against his broad chest, his hips leaning back against the kitchen bench, silently watching her with his I've-got-all-the-time-in-the-world pose. And then she would blurt out everything, all the hurt, all the shame of not being able to cope, the sheer terror of reliving it all. And then the nightmares would begin again, and then the panic attacks, and the zombie-like days when it was all she could do to get out of bed, let alone out of the house.

Fran pulled her shoulders back, her neck protesting as she locked gazes with him. 'I'm not prepared to commit myself to anything until I have thought it through. I am supposed to be having an extended holiday as well as looking after my sister. I haven't even visited her in hospital yet. Pelican Bay will have to do without me, Sergeant Hawke, as I have other priorities right now.'

Fran was proud of her speech. She had made it sound so in control and assured, so nothing-you-can-say-will-sway-me. But then he came around the island bench where she was standing and stood right in front of her, invading her personal space, making every shallow breath she took bring her breasts almost into intimate contact with his chest. She had never been more acutely aware of her body or, in fact, anyone else's.

Every nerve was jangling, fizzing with sensation beneath her skin. Her nostrils filled with the primal male scent of him, the warmth of his body and the late-day perspiration that should have repelled her but for some reason did exactly the opposite.

Her eyes went to his mouth, her tongue darting out to wet them in case he kissed her. Her heart gave an almighty thump. *Was* he going to kiss her? Oh, God, she should have brushed her teeth while she'd had the chance. She should have at the very least rinsed with mouthwash. But, then, she'd just had a sip or two of coffee so—

'I want you to think about something, Dr Nin,' he said in a gravel-rough tone that made her skin lift all over.

She swallowed, not just a tiny swallow, but a melon-sized one. 'Y-yes?'

His arctic eyes were like ice picks pinning hers. 'When you drive up to visit your sister, I hope for your sake each and every one of the towns you pass through has a qualified doctor in residence in case you happen to need medical assistance along the way.'

Fran blinked, she thought it was probably for the first time in a whole minute, maybe longer. 'Are you planning on riding that motorbike of yours any time soon on the same roads I will be using?' she asked in an arch tone.

His eyes wrestled with hers but she refused to give in. She held him stare for stare, her heart beating so fast it felt like the percussion sections from three orchestras had taken up residence inside her chest.

After what seemed a week he stepped away from her. Picking up his police hat from the seat of one of the kitchen stools where he'd placed it earlier, he put it on his head, so low it shielded his eyes. 'If I do I will be making a special effort to keep an eye out for you,' he said with a hint of mockery in his tone.

Fran kept her mouth tightly closed, watching as he strode to the door, her stomach feeling hollow when the door clicked shut on his exit.

Rufus tilted his head from side to side in doggy confusion, a soft whine that sounded so mournful Fran glared at him. 'Don't you start,' she said, and then as he gave her a hangdog look she sank to the floor and, wrapping her arms around his shaggy neck, hugged him close. 'Sorry,' she said, wondering why she felt so close to tears.

CHAPTER FOUR

'OH, MY gosh, they're absolutely gorgeous!' Fran breathed as she looked through the neonatal nursery window at tiny Joshua and Timmy.

'Timmy's still having some trouble breathing on his own,' Caro said. 'They're still not sure if he will need to go to Sydney but so far so good. But Joshua's doing well. I was able to feed him with some expressed milk earlier.' She gave a heavy sigh and added, 'I just wish I could take them both home right now.'

Fran tucked her arm through her sister's. 'Hang in there, Caro,' she said. 'You need to concentrate on the twins' health right now and, anyway, everything's fine at home.'

'Yes, thanks to you it is,' Caro said as they made their way back to her room on the ward. 'I ran into Jane Pelleri in the hospital cafeteria. You saved little Ella's life. Everyone's talking about it and about how you helped Candi Broderick after her fall off her horse. You didn't mention a word to me or Nick last time we spoke. Why not?'

'I didn't want to worry you both,' Fran said. *And because I didn't actually save Ella's life.* 'You'd just had the boys and it all happened so fast in any case.'

Caro gave her a big sister I'm-older-and-wiser look. 'But doesn't that tell you something?'

Fran blew out a breath. 'Look, it you're going to join Sergeant Hawke's mission to have me settle in Pelican Bay as the local GP, forget it. The right person for the job will come along soon enough and I am definitely not it.'

'But what if you *are* the right person, Fran?'

Fran screwed up her mouth. 'If I was, then the town—as they say in those old westerns—is not going to be big enough for both of us.'

Caro's brows lifted and her eyes twinkled. 'So it's pistols at dawn with Sergeant Hawke, is it?'

Fran flicked her hair back behind her shoulders. 'I can't remember when I've met a more annoying man. He gets under my skin. I think he does it deliberately. And then I find out he's just lost his mother after a long illness and I felt such a fool for shouting at him for cutting me off that day because apparently he'd just got the call and was rushing to get back, but how was I supposed to know that? He never said a word. In fact no one said a word. I would have apologised then and there but he never said a thing. Then he came around for coffee and just stood there, making me feel uncomfortable. I can't seem to win with him. I don't know why he's so...so *infuriating*!'

'Gosh, I'm sorry. I should have told you about his mother but the twins arriving early totally distracted me.'

Fran gawped at her sister. 'You knew?'

Caro winced. 'Sorry, but Beryl told me he wanted it kept pretty quiet. I think only she and Jim Broderick knew about it until a day or so ago.'

Fran flicked her eyes upwards in frustration. 'You could have told me. I made a complete and utter fool of myself.'

'Ah-h…' Caro sighed.

Fran gave her sister a beady look. 'What was that sigh for?'

Caro's expression was guileless. 'What sigh?'

'You know what sigh,' Fran said, scowling. 'That big sister-I-know-something-you-don't-know sigh.'

'What would it hurt to give Jacob's suggestion a try?' Caro asked.

Fran narrowed her eyes. 'How do you know about Sergeant Hawke's suggestion?'

Caro pointed to the two little blue teddy bears dressed in football jerseys propped up next to a bunch of flowers on her bedside table. 'Because he ran into Nick downstairs about an hour before you did. I was in the nursery, feeding the bubs, so I didn't actually speak to him personally. He was on his way to a court case in Sydney and dropped in on his way through. Nick told me Jacob thought you should put in some hours at the clinic. It sounds like a great idea, don't you think?'

Fran pursed her lips so tightly they felt like they were stitched in place.

'It's not like anyone's asking you to do it full time,' her sister went on. 'Just a day or two a week for a couple of hours, four at the most, until a new locum is found.'

Fran turned to look out of the window, her shoulders hunched, her arms crossed over her chest. 'Did Nick tell him what happened?' she asked when she could trust herself to speak.

'Of course he didn't!' Caro sounded wounded. 'A promise is a promise, even if both Nick and I think it's a totally stupid one.'

Fran rolled her eyes again. 'It's not stupid to me. I want to rebuild my life my way with no one looking at me with pity in their eyes.'

'Jacob's a cop, Frannie,' Caro said. 'He's probably had to deal with the same stuff you did lots of times in his career. I bet he's had lots of drug addicts throw punches and kicks at him, maybe even pull a knife on him or even worse—a gun. I reckon he's the one person in town who would understand what you've been through.'

Fran limped over to where she had placed her handbag earlier and hoisted it over her shoulder. 'No one can do that, Carolyn,' she said bitterly. 'The day Scott Draper attacked me I changed and I can't change back. No amount of understanding is going to do that.'

'You're letting him win, don't you see that?' Caro said. 'You're letting a drunken drug addict who didn't even know what he was doing at the time take your life away from you.'

'Don't lecture me on what I should do,' Fran said tightly, feeling her emotions bubbling up inside her at the injustice of it all. 'You weren't there. You don't know what it was like.'

'You have to put it behind you, Fran,' Caro insisted. 'Mum and Dad put their lives on hold for you for three months while you got back on your feet. Now it's your turn to do your bit to aid your recovery. You have to put in an effort. I know it's hard, honey. But I'm here for you and the whole of Pelican Bay will support you if you would let them know about it, I just know they would.'

Fran knew some of what her sister said was right. Her parents had lived every day of the month she had been in an induced coma not knowing whether their youngest daughter would ever breathe on her own again, let alone practise medicine again. They had helped her through the long, slow rehabilitation process, every day helping her get to and from physiotherapy sessions, tirelessly supporting her until she was able to regain her independence.

It had been just as hard for Caro, living miles away with her husband, travelling back and forth during the first gruelling months of her pregnancy to visit her, doing what she could to help.

'I know at some point I will have to move on,' Fran said, letting her bag slip from her shoulder as she came over to her sister's bed. 'I know I have to put the past behind me. I just have to. But I'm scared.' She buried her head into the soft pillow of her sister's chest, sighing as Caro's arms wrapped around her. 'I'm so scared I won't be able to be the same competent doctor I was before.'

She lifted her head to meet her sister's gaze. 'I nearly lost that child, Caro. I didn't save her, Jacob did. I totally froze and if it hadn't been for Jacob taking over…' She shuddered and added in a hoarse whisper, 'I'm just so scared it will happen again and there won't be anyone around to help me.'

Caro stroked Fran's hair, cuddling her close with her other arm. 'I know you are scared, sweetie, but one step at a time, OK?'

It was a long while before Fran lifted her head again to look at her sister. 'I'd better get going. Rufus has probably eaten his way through the sofa and the coffee tables by now.'

Caro smiled. 'I think he's well on his way to falling in love with you.'

Fran got off the bed and picked up her bag, digging for her keys inside it. 'Yeah, well, a dog is a great companion and all that, but it would be nice if I could get a decent man to do the same.'

'I wasn't talking about Rufus.'

Fran's fingers closed around her keys, her chest feeling as if her hand was doing the very same thing to her heart. 'You're imagining things, Caro,' she said, avoiding her sister's all-seeing gaze. 'The man is hardly civil to me. He thinks I'm a lazy layabout city chick with nothing better to do than to work on my tan between skiing holidays.'

'He's quite a catch, Fran,' Caro said. 'And much better looking than anyone you've dated in the past.'

Fran tried to bring some of past boyfriends' features to mind but it was a bit of a blur, although she didn't think she should tell her sister that. It sounded so shallow of her to not even be able to picture even one of them mentally, especially as there had only been three and only one of them had been relatively serious.

'Jacob Hawke's OK, I guess,' she said in an offhand tone. 'But he rides a donor cycle which is a definite strike against him.'

Caro's forehead became a road map of fine lines. 'A donor cycle? What the hell is a donor cycle?'

'It's what A and E doctors call motorbikes,' Fran answered. 'I always swore after I did a term in neurosurgery when I was a registrar that I would never get involved with a man who rode a motorbike. Head injuries are so common. It's too dangerous.'

'Maybe he likes to live a little dangerously,' Caro said, her eyes glinting mischievously. 'I think he looks amazingly sexy in his police uniform, and when he's in all that black leather riding gear it makes me think of—'

'Don't.' Fran held up her hand like a stop sign. 'I'm off men at the moment, remember?'

Caro gave her a knowing look. 'Frannie, you've always been off men. All through your teens you were totally focussed on studying. And then all through med school and ever since you qualified work was always more important to you, more's the pity. A casual love affair with a handsome cop is just what you need right now to boost your confidence.'

Fran hoisted her handbag strap over her shoulder. 'I hope to God you didn't get Nick to suggest such a thing to Sergeant Hawke,' she said.

'Would I do that?' Caro said with that same twinkling smile.

When Fran went to the general store the following day she ran into Jane Pelleri, who was doing a quick shop while her husband looked after the children. Ella was now back at home, showing no sign of any after-effects from her terrifying experience. The pool gate had been repaired and life was more or less back to normal. So different from so many others, Fran thought as she listened to Jane recount something cute the boys had done to welcome their baby sister home.

Beryl Hadley wasn't working on the cash register that day but a slim, almost thin young girl of about sixteen was filling in for her. Fran smiled as she loaded her things on the counter but the teenager barely looked up as she mechanically scanned the items. She was dressed in loose-fitting black clothes—even the top she was wearing was long sleeved which must have been sweltering for her in spite of the air-conditioning inside.

'Hi, I'm Fran, Carolyn Atkins's sister,' Fran said to break the silence. 'Is Beryl having a day off?'

'Yeah.' The girl scanned the packet of dog treats Fran had chosen for Rufus.

'What's your name?' Fran asked after another few items were scanned. 'I don't think I've seen you around town before.'

'Tara,' she said dully, scanning the last item and bringing up the total. 'Will that be cash or charge?'

Fran handed over some notes. When the girl placed the change in her hand Fran noticed several thin white scars on the underside of the teenager's wrist. The girl pulled her sleeve back in place and closed the drawer of the cash register with one of her bony hips.

'Nice to meet you, Tara,' Fran said, picking up her bags.

'Yeah,' Tara said without meeting Fran's gaze. 'Same.'

Fran was coming out of the store, still frowning, when a man in his early sixties approached her. 'Dr Nin,' he said. 'I'm so glad to meet you at last. I'm Nigel McLeod, the mayor.'

'Pleased to meet you, Mr McLeod,' Fran said, juggling her shopping bags to shake his proffered hand.

'I was wondering if you would like to have a tour of the medical clinic this morning,' he said. 'Everyone is so thrilled about how you stepped into the breach, so to speak.'

Fran took a step backwards. 'Um…I haven't exactly said I—'

'It's just such an amazing coincidence,' he went on as if she hadn't spoken. 'It's obviously meant to be. Here we are waiting desperately for the position to be filled since the GP who was supposed to arrive has had some doubts cast over his overseas qualifications and then you turn up. It's a miracle, that's what it is. An answer to a prayer and, believe you me, this whole town has been praying for someone as competent as you. The way you saved that little girl's life and Jim Broderick's daughter too. The orthopaedic doctor at the hospital she was flown to said she was lucky she didn't lose that leg. You're Pelican Bay's latest hero. I am sure you'll be nominated as citizen of the year after this.'

Fran gave him a wan smile. 'Mr McLeod…I am very grateful for your offer but I'm not planning on—'

'Of course I know it's a dreadful imposition but there are already several patients lined up to see you,' he said. 'As soon as they heard there was a doctor in town, they booked in. Linda Brew is the clinic receptionist. She's been on the phone, fielding calls all morning. Oh, to be so popular!' He beamed. 'I wish it worked like that for me when it came to council elections.'

Fran's smile turned to a grimace. She could see worming her way out of this was going to take more flexibility than that of an Olympic gymnast. She thought of the patients who had their hopes up, probably already sitting there on the edges of the waiting room chairs, eagerly anticipating her attendance. What if one of them was like Jacob's mother, in desperate need of pain relief? How could she say no? It wasn't as if a drug-crazed maniac was going to barge through the doors out here. This was Pelican Bay, a quiet seaside village, not the centre of Melbourne's nightclub scene. The sort of stuff she would be dealing with here would be things like chickenpox, for example, or chest infections, the occasional laceration, maybe some broken bones like Candi Broderick's, but hopefully no more near-drownings like little Ella Pelleri's. Maybe she could do it as a once-off, a sort of favour to the town, but that was all.

'Look, Mr McLeod, I'm not making any promises or anything, but since there are patients already wait—'

'So we'll expect you at, say…' Nigel McLeod checked his watch '…ten-thirty?'

She nodded in resignation, a sigh escaping her lips. 'Ten-thirty it is.'

Fran put her shopping in the boot of her car but didn't notice the parking infringement ticket tucked under her left-hand windscreen wiper until she was behind the wheel with the engine already running.

She sucked in a breath and got out of the car. Limping across, she snatched up the ticket, peering at the officer's signature at the bottom. The handwriting was virtually impossible to read, but she could make out an H and a K without any difficulty. She seethed with anger as she got back behind the wheel. She had just enough time to take her shopping back to the house before going down to the station to have it out with Sergeant Jacob Hawke.

'You have a visitor, Sarg,' Nathan Jeffrey announced via the intercom.

'Who is it?' Jacob asked as he lifted the ice pack off his eye, wincing when he saw he was still bleeding high on his cheekbone.

He hadn't expected Wayne Clark to be quite so aggressive about his bald tyres.

Jacob knew things were tough on some of the locals who tried to make a living off the land backing onto the bay. Wayne was one of them. The rain that fell on the coast didn't always fall on the hinterland. Like Jim Broderick, Wayne had lost his wife, not from death but from desertion to another man, leaving him with a son who had a record of petty crime and a daughter who had played truant more days from school than she had attended during the last term.

'Dr Nin,' Nathan said.

Jacob gave an inward groan. That was just what he needed right now. 'Send her in,' he said, holding the pack to his throbbing eye again.

Fran stepped into the office and frowned when she saw the ice pack on Jacob's face. 'What happened to you?' she asked.

He looked at her with one steely eye. 'Nothing that should concern you since you're so determined not to practise medicine.'

She gave him a slitted-eye look. 'Which you have very cleverly circumvented by making it virtually impossible for me to refuse to conduct at least one clinic, if not more.'

He leaned back in his chair, the ice pack on his eye like a pirate patch. 'I take it our hard-working mayor, Nigel McLeod, has been putting the hard word on you.'

She planted her hands on her hips. 'No doubt at your command.'

He leaned forward in his chair. 'I had nothing to do with it.'

She stared at him, her mouth set in a tight line. 'I don't believe you.'

He leaned back and pressed the pack even more firmly against his eye. 'This town needs a doctor but if you feel you're not up to the task then that's fine. The last thing we need around here is someone who is less than enthusiastic or—worse—lacking in confidence.'

Fran bristled, trying to hold on to her temper. 'I *will* do the clinic but only once and only because there are patients waiting there for me, not because you've engineered it.'

He put the ice pack on his desk. 'I had nothing to do with engineering anything.'

She tried to stare him down but she couldn't help noticing how the cut on his cheekbone just below his eye was seeping a slow but steady trickle of blood. He was going to have a bruiser, if she was any judge.

'How did you get that?' she asked.

'One of the perks of the job,' he quipped. 'Believe me, today has been a good day.'

She rolled her eyes before she could stop the impulse. 'You should get that checked. It might need stitching.'

He leaned back even further in his chair, the leather creaking in protest. 'It's just a scratch,' he said, reapplying the cold pack as he crossed one ankle over his muscular thigh. 'Now, what did you want to see me about?'

Fran slapped the parking infringement notice on the desk

in front of him. 'If this is how you do things around here then you're going exactly the wrong way about convincing me to commit to this community,' she said. 'I didn't expect a police officer of your rank to be so petty.'

His eyes briefly scanned the notice before meeting hers. 'You do the crime, Dr Nin, you pay the fine.'

She ground her teeth and, snatching up the notice, tore it into shreds, letting them scatter like snowflakes on his desk. 'So book me, Sergeant Hawke,' she challenged him.

Jacob put the ice pack on his desk and, pushing back his chair, got to his feet. 'You seem pretty convinced I wrote that ticket,' he said, holding her stormy gaze.

She curled her top lip at him. 'You're going to deny it?'

'I am not the only cop in town, Dr Nin,' he reminded her.

She tilted her chin, her eyes still flashing at him. 'Maybe so, but I bet there isn't another J. Hawke, is there?'

'No, there's not,' he said. 'There is, however, a John Hank.'

Her blue-grey eyes widened for a second before dropping to the little snowstorm on his desk. 'Oh…'

'I can ask him to show you the duplicate,' Jacob offered. 'But either way, if you parked in the wrong zone you need to pay the fine.'

Her eyes slowly came back to his, her tongue sweeping over her lips in a tell-tale movement of discomfiture. 'I—I'm sorry,' she said. 'It's just when I saw the J and the H and the K, I assumed it was your signature.'

'It's an easy mistake to make,' he acknowledged.

Her eyes went to the shredded ticket on his desk again. Taking a deep breath, she stepped forward. 'I'll clean this up for you. It won't take a—'

Jacob put his hand down over her smaller one, pinning it to the desk. 'Leave it.'

Fran looked into his unusual blue eyes, her heart giving a little stumble. She glanced down at the desk. His hand dwarfed hers, his long fingers warm and dry and determined. Her mind began to wander…to imagine how it would feel to have his long, strong body pinning hers beneath his, to have his warm, beautifully sculpted mouth feasting hungrily on hers, to have his hands shape her breasts, each one in turn, exploring the tightly budded nipples, bringing his hot, moist mouth down, licking, stroking, sucking on her until she writhed with pleasure.

'Um…I should go now…' she said, trying to slide her fingers out from under his. *Like right now.*

'Wait.' The pressure of his hand was firm but not brutally so.

Fran could feel the slightly rougher skin on the pads of his fingers, as if he was no stranger to manual work. She suddenly thought of each of her past boyfriends, none of whom had seemed able to change a toilet roll, let alone a tyre.

Sergeant Jacob Hawke looked the sort of man who could do just about anything, like make her think thoughts she had no right to be thinking. Dangerous thoughts, thoughts of furnace-hot kisses and sensually stroking hands…

'Forget about the parking fine,' he said. 'I'll sort it out with Senior Constable Hank.'

She looked back into his eyes, her lips feeling as if his dark-rimmed gaze had scorched the moist surface of her mouth. God knew what would happen if his lips touched hers, she thought, glancing at his mouth as the tip of her tongue quickly darted out to moisten her own. She would probably sizzle like a fried egg on a hot tin roof.

'Er…that's very kind of you,' she said. 'But I don't mind paying my dues, really. It's the law, as you say, and I did stay a bit longer than the time on the sign…or at least only a couple of minutes but I'm used to parking meters in the city so I guess things are different down…down…here…'

Fran lost track of what she was saying. The cut on his cheek had stopped bleeding but she could see the slight swelling around his eye, a hint of a bruise already making its way to the surface of his tanned skin.

'Um…would you like me to dress that for you?' she asked. 'It's stopped bleeding but it probably needs cleansing to avoid infection.'

'There's no need,' he said, removing his hand from hers. 'I'll see to it myself.'

'Fine then,' she said, readjusting her handbag strap on her shoulder as she stepped back from the desk on legs that felt like those of a string puppet's. 'I'm…er…sorry to have taken up so much of your time.'

'Not at all.'

There was a silence, broken only by the sound of the clock ticking on the wall behind Jacob's desk.

Tick.

Tick.

Tick.

'Do you fancy a drink after work this evening?' he asked.

Fran blinked. 'Um…pardon?'

'A drink at the pub after work,' he said. 'You and me and two glasses, usually with something alcoholic in them, but it's not mandatory—the alcohol, I mean.'

She continued to stare at him. 'You're…you're asking me on a…on a date?'

His expression and his tone seemed to communicate a take-it-or-leave-it attitude, which irked her.

The last thing she needed was a date with a man she didn't

even like. Attractive he might be, but unlike some of her peers she was not interested in casual dates to fill in the time. She could just imagine what he would expect from her at the end of the evening, but that was one game she wasn't going to play. Perhaps he thought she was desperate for a date on account of her limp. When she'd first come out of hospital a workman had called out something rude to her as she'd hobbled past a building site on her crutches, and ever since she had struggled with her self-esteem, seeing every man's interest as pity rather than genuine interest.

Fran straightened to her full height which, without heels, meant she had to crick her neck to meet his gaze. 'Actually, I am busy tonight,' she said, and stood there, waiting for him to suggest the following night, but he said nothing.

The ensuing silence throbbed for several seconds, as if an invisible finger had reached up and stopped the second hand on the clock.

Fran felt the heat begin to crawl like a slow-moving tide from her neck to her cheeks. 'Um…I'd better go,' she said. 'I apparently have patients waiting for me.'

He gave a nod without saying anything, his arms now folded against his chest, his hips leaning against the filing cabinet, the gunbelt around his lean waist like a menacing third presence in the room.

'Have a nice day, Sergeant Hawke,' she said as she turned to leave.

He didn't say a word.

Not a *single* word.

Damn him.

Triple damn him.

Fran closed the door and walked past Nathan Jeffery with a stiff smile pasted on her face. 'Have a nice day, Constable.'

'You too, Dr Nin,' he said with a friendly smile. 'It's great you're filling in down at the clinic, by the way. My girlfriend is booked in to see you this morning.'

'I'll look forward to meeting her,' Fran said, and with another tight smile left.

As soon as Fran turned off the engine outside the clinic she felt her body break out in a cold sweat. She looked at her hands where they were still gripping the steering-wheel, each of her knuckles looking like they were going to break through her skin. She tried to control her breathing, in and out, slowly, thinking of peaceful, calming things, but nothing helped. She felt nauseous, hot and clammy and, winding down the window, she gulped in some fresh air.

Still sitting inside the car, she looked at the clinic, taking in its cottage-like appearance, which should have been of some comfort but unfortunately wasn't. The clinic was painted white with grey trim and a small recently painted white picket fence surrounded the block, A peppercorn tree provided some shade on one side and a wattle tree on the other. There was a pair of magpies chortling to each other in the wattle tree and a soldier bird was picking at some crumbs near the rubbish bin at the side of the cottage. It was as far away from a frantically busy city A and E department as could be, and yet Fran's heart was beating like a drum in staccato.

After a few more minutes she opened the car door and eased her legs out, taking her time, mentally taking the steps to the front door.

She could do this.

It would be hard but she could do it.

She had to start somewhere. This was going to be a lot easier than a busy city hospital. Way easier.

As she stood, waiting for her legs to steady enough to negotiate the pathway to the front door of the clinic, she saw a police car take the corner at breakneck speed, the blue light flashing and the siren blazing as the vehicle sped past the clinic, whipping up a cloud of dust in its wake.

The flashing lights and piercing siren of the volunteer fire engine that came around the same corner at a slightly lower speed did nothing to help Fran's already jittery nerves. Her brain exploded with flashbacks, zigzags of light blinded her, she could hear raised voices, screaming voices, one louder and higher and more terrified than the rest. And then there were the footsteps racing down the corridor, squeaky nurses' shoes, and heavy ones…

She clutched at her chest where her heart seemed to be intent on pushing its way out of her body, her eyes clamped shut against the images that haunted her.

Breathe.

All she had to do was breathe and it would all pass…

'Dr Nin?' a female voice called out to her from the pavement.

Fran opened her eyes and vaguely registered a middle-aged woman looking at her with wide-eyed concern. 'I—I'm sorry,' she said, swallowing back nausea. 'I…I have the most appalling headache. I…I won't be able to do the clinic… I'm so sorry…'

She stumbled back to the car and got behind the wheel in a tangle of limbs that was as ungainly as it was painful.

The clinic receptionist—or at least that was who Fran assumed it was by the uniform and name badge the woman was wearing—rushed to the driver's door. 'Do you really think you should be driving, Dr Nin?' she asked, frowning. 'I can get someone to take you home if you like.'

'No... Please,' Fran insisted, pulling down the seat belt, strangely comforted by the security it offered in her disordered state. 'I'm fine. It's not far. I wouldn't have driven at all except...well... I'm sorry... I have to go...'

'You take care of yourself, dear,' Linda Brew said, patting the window panel. 'The patients will understand. I'll make another booking for another day. How about tomorrow, is that all right?'

Fran was beyond thinking of going through all this again and mumbled something in reply as she started the car. She backed out and drove back to Caro's house as slowly as she could without drawing too much attention to herself.

Rufus greeted her with a puzzled look when she came through the door. Fran gave his ears a ruffle with a hand that was still clammy and trembling.

And then she crawled like an injured child into her darkened bedroom, huddling up into the foetal position, rocking and rocking until the sobs that racked her chest slowly subsided.

CHAPTER FIVE

WHEN Fran woke up it was still light, the afternoon sun slanting in through a gap in the curtains. Rufus was standing by her bed, wagging his tail, his brown marble-like eyes beseeching.

'I suppose you would like a walk, right?' she asked, hauling herself upright and shoving the bird's nest of her hair away from her face.

Rufus barked and wagged his tail so hard he knocked off the newly framed photo of the twins she had put on the bedside table. 'Come on, then,' she said, putting her shoes on, wincing as her leg protested after being still for so long.

As she walked along the beach with Rufus, she found herself going the extra distance to the rock pools, rationalising that it was purely for Rufus's sake as he had been locked up in the house for most of the day. Of course, it wasn't exactly for Rufus's sake that she covertly peered up the cliff to make out Jacob's home.

The house was certainly well hidden by the bush surrounding it, but she could just make out the bank of windows that overlooked the bay. She shielded her eyes with one hand and angled her gaze to see if she could see anyone moving about.

The trees were swaying in the slight breeze, giving her an occasional glimpse of the timber frame of the house but nothing else.

'Are you looking for me?' a deep male voice said from behind her.

Fran's heart jumped. She spun around but because of the weakness in her leg she lost her balance. She felt herself teetering but the iron brace of Jacob's hands on her upper arms steadied her, holding her as he looked down at her, his body so close to hers she could feel his warmth.

'Y-you gave me such a fright,' she said, breathing heavily from residual panic. Of course, it had nothing to do with the fact he was wearing nothing but his running shorts and shoes, neither did it have anything to do with the steely grip of his fingers on her arms and how close she was standing to him.

'Sorry,' he said, releasing her, 'but you were looking rather intently up there. I was sure you must have wanted to see me about something.'

Fran rubbed at her arms for a moment but the skin still tingled where his hands had pressed. 'No, I was…er…just going for a walk.'

He gave her a long and probing look. 'Headache all gone?'

Fran compressed her lips, forcing herself to hold his gaze. 'How do you know I had a headache?'

'Linda Brew at the clinic told me,' he said. 'I called in there on my way past to find you had cancelled a full list of patients. That must have been some headache.'

Fran tightened her mouth even further. 'It was.'

'You know,' he said, still looking at her in that penetrating way of his, 'if you really would prefer to sun yourself on the beach, maybe you should go somewhere else where no one knows you're a doctor. If you pull that sort of stunt once too often around here, you're going to tick off a lot of people.'

'Maybe I *will* go somewhere else,' Fran said stiffly, and turned to look for Rufus but there was no sign of him.

'Rufus?' she called, and began to scan the beach, her heart starting to move from a canter to a gallop when there was response. 'Where can he have got to? He was here just a minute or two ago.'

'He won't be far away. He's probably picked up a scent and gone after it.'

'I hope you're right,' she said, frowning in worry. 'Caro will kill me if anything happens to that dog.'

Jacob gave a whistle, waited and then repeated it.

Fran strained her ears to listen above the sound of the waves crashing against the shore. 'Did you hear that?' she asked as she picked up the faint sound of a bark.

'Yeah,' Jacob said, reaching for her hand. 'Come on, I think I know where he is.'

Fran hesitated for a second before she slipped her hand into his, her stomach dropping another two floors as his fingers wrapped around hers. She had held hands with her last boyfriend for weeks and not once had her arm fizzed like it was doing now. It wasn't the first time she had thought it, and she was almost certain it wasn't going to be the last, but if that was what Jacob's touch felt like, what on earth would it be like to be kissed by him?

'There's a small cave behind that rockfall over there,' Jacob said as he helped Fran over the rocks. 'The main network of caves was cut off when that part of the cliff came down just after the Second World War. There's been no restoration work conducted as the caves were never considered all that safe for public use.'

Fran was glad of the strength of his grip as she navigated the rough terrain. 'Do you think that's where Rufus has gone?' she asked once she was back on level ground.

Jacob released her hand and pointed to the grassy fringe at the base of the cliff. 'You can see where the rabbits have been around here,' he said. 'My guess is he's chased one into the cave.'

She looked at the tiny opening of the cave, barely visible through the scrubby growth. 'How will we get him out?'

He gave her a brief unreadable glance before he looked back at the opening. 'Good question.'

Fran tucked her windswept hair behind one shoulder. 'I guess you've probably already guessed he's not the most obedient dog.'

'It might not be a matter of obedience, getting him out,' he said, crouching down to separate the overgrown scrub. 'If he's gone in too far he might have become trapped. God knows what the condition of the other caves is like in there after all these years. Give him another call and let's see if he responds.'

Fran called Rufus a couple of times, giving Jacob a what-do-we-do-now look when there was no response, not even a scuffle or a whine. 'Maybe he's not in there after all,' she said hopefully.

Jacob picked a piece of rust-coloured shaggy dog hair off one of the bushes and held it up to her to inspect.

Her shoulders went down. 'Oh…'

'Don't worry,' he said, working at the entrance again. 'He might just be out of hearing. I'll give him another whistle.'

Fran watched as he cleared away the scrub, the muscles of his back and shoulders contracting under his tanned skin. He was in superb condition, not a gram of fat on him anywhere. It made her want to slide the palms of her hands over him to see if he felt as good as he looked.

'Did you hear that?' he asked.

She looked at him blankly for a moment, her hands still mentally exploring his taut buttocks. 'Um…no…I didn't…'

'He's definitely in there,' Jacob said, springing to his feet with the sort of agility Fran could only envy. 'Will you be all right here for a few minutes? I'm going to run up to the house to get a torch and some gear.'

'Yes, of course.'

She watched him jog back up the beach to the pathway leading to his house until he disappeared. She turned back to the cave's entrance and bent down to peer into the blackness. 'Rufus?' she called out. 'Rufus?'

She heard it this time, a muffled bark of distress that made her stomach curdle with fear. 'Are you all right?' she asked even as she thought, What a stupid question. The poor mutt could hardly answer her but somehow she felt he would like to know there was someone there to help him.

It seemed no time at all before Jacob was back. Fran turned as he rock-hopped his way to her, carrying a hard hat, torch, a pair of overalls and a rope.

'Let me guess,' she said. 'You've done this sort of search and rescue before.'

He gave her a ghost of a smile, making her ache to see more. 'Yeah, you could say that.' He stepped into the overalls and did up the press-lock buttons up the front, before placing the hard hat on his head.

He uncoiled the rope with a clip attached to the end and, moving past Fran, tied it securely to a tree a few feet away, tugging on it to check it held.

'You're going in?' she asked, wincing as she thought of the spiders and sticky cobwebs.

'I won't be able to go very far,' he said, and clipped the

other end of the rope to the belt on his overalls. 'It'll be a bit of a squeeze but I should be able to see far enough inside to work out where Rufus is.'

Fran was embarrassed at the trouble her sister's dog had caused, but was also secretly pleased to watch Jacob in action. There was something incredibly attractive about a man's man, the sort of man who was not afraid of a bit of dirt and dust, not afraid of the unknown, just determined to get the job done, whatever it took. She supposed it was part of his training as a cop. He had that aura of command about him. Cool under pressure, calm in the face of adversity. Dependable, dedicated…deliciously male and—

Fran had to shake herself out of her reverie when Jacob backed out of the cave entrance, asking for Rufus's lead. She crouched down beside his long legs and passed it to him. 'Can you see him?' she asked.

'Yes,' he said as he moved back into the cave. 'It looks like he's dropped down a crevice.'

Fran felt her insides clench. 'Is he hurt?'

'It's hard to tell,' he answered. 'Ah…I can see him better now. No, he looks fine. Just a bit shocked, I think. Hey, boy. What are you doing down there?'

Fran let out a breath of relief when she heard an answering whine. She watched as Jacob wriggled some more, this time leaving just his ankles and feet out of the cave as he reached down into the crevice and clipped on Rufus's lead.

Within a few dusty seconds both man and dog were outside, Rufus looking distinctly cowed after his adventure and Jacob looking…well…gorgeous, Fran decided. He had a cobweb draped on each broad shoulder and a smear of dust over his right cheek, and the graze above his cheekbone had started bleeding again from being scratched by something.

She had never seen a more heart-stopping sight.

'I don't know how to thank you,' she said as she took Rufus's lead.

Jacob used his forearm to mop the sweat from his brow. 'No problem.'

Fran's eyes were automatically drawn to a mark on his arm. 'Your arm…' She peered closer. 'It looks like it's been burnt.'

'Yeah, I got that when I was out helping at the fire in the valley. Old Jack McBride was doing some brush-cutting and a spark lit a scrub fire. A branch came down and I wasn't quick enough to get out of the way.'

'But it needs dressing,' she said, frowning up at him. 'Burns are notorious for getting infected and you've just been crawling around in a dusty cave.'

He gave her a wry look. 'Yeah, well, I would have if there had been a doctor on duty at the clinic. I called past but Linda told me you had shot through with a headache.'

Fran bit her lip, shifting her weight from foot to foot. The way he had said the word 'headache' felt like he had lifted his fingers in quotation marks for emphasis. That he didn't believe her story about the headache was as clear as the cobwebs hanging from his shoulders.

For the want of something to fill the awkward silence she said, 'Um…you have cobwebs on your shoulders…'

He gave them a quick brush off his overalls and took off his hat. 'I felt something go down the back of my neck but it might have just been a bit of dust.'

Fran watched as he stepped out of the overalls, her stomach giving a little flutter of awareness as his bronzed flesh came into view. He had a light dusting of chest hair, covering both pectoral muscles, narrowing down the flat plane of his stomach, finally disappearing below the waistband of his shorts. Her imagination did the rest and it made her heart race as a result.

'Anything there?' he asked, turning his back to her to inspect.

Fran swept her gaze over his taut frame, marvelling again at the breadth of his shoulders and the narrowness of his waist and hips. 'Er…no…there's nothing there…' she said over a ridge in her throat.

He turned back to face her. 'Do you think you could manage the pathway up to my place?' he asked.

Fran would never have admitted it even if she couldn't. 'Sure, but there's no need to—'

'Hey, I saved your sister's dog,' he said with that almost-there smile. 'Doesn't that mean you owe me in some way? Besides, you can dress my burn for me as you were indisposed earlier.'

She pursed her lips, even though her stomach gave that little flutter of excitement again at being with him—alone. 'I guess I do owe you something for Rufus's sake…'

He scooped up his gear and, tucking it under one arm, reached for Rufus's lead with the other. 'Let me take him,' he said. 'You go first and then if you lose your footing I'll be able to stop you from slipping all the way down.'

'You make it sound quite perilous,' Fran said as she made her way carefully over the rocks.

He kept a few paces back, keeping Rufus well out of her way. 'It's just a bit rough and overgrown in spots but I don't want to cut it back as it keeps trespassers away.'

Fran was conscious of her limp as she started on the path, conscious, too, of the fact that Jacob had a clear and uninter-rupted view of her behind all the way to the top. It was a little unnerving to think about a full-blooded man's gaze on her, especially Jacob's. Something about him made her aware of her body in a way she hadn't been in months. She had seen the way his eyes had swept over her on the beach, taking in her light skirt and close-fitting top. Her skin had felt as if he had touched her with those long calloused fingers, making every fine hair on her body stand up erect, like soldiers at drill practice.

Lost in her thoughts, Fran planted her foot between two rocks but somehow caught the edge of one. She wobbled for a moment and just as she thought she was going to go down, Jacob's hands settled on her waist.

'Whoa there,' he said, the warmth of his body behind her like a protective shield. 'Take it easy.'

Fran breathed in the scent of him, the earthy male scent that made the blood start to race in her veins. She had only to lean back and she would feel every hard plane of his body against hers. The temptation to do so was almost overwhelming, and if it hadn't been for the steep incline and the presence of Rufus, Fran knew she might very well have given into it. 'I—I'm fine…' she said a little breathlessly.

His hands slowly released her. 'It's a bit clearer up ahead, not so many rocks.'

Fran continued on, stopping at one point to look at a gecko that was making the most of the afternoon sun. 'Have you seen any snakes along here?' she asked.

'One or two,' he said. 'More see you than you see them, of course. They can get pretty aggressive during the mating season in February, but only if you disturb them.'

The bush opened up in front of them and Fran got her first full glimpse of Jacob's house. It was a simple design, large windows and a wrap-around deck that would be perfect for lazy afternoons, sipping tea, relaxing and taking in the view.

'Have you bought this or are you renting?' she asked as he led the way inside.

'I bought it,' Jacob said. 'Even if I move on at some point I figured it was too good a location to miss out on. My parents honeymooned in Pelican Bay thirty-five years ago. Back then there wasn't even a general store. I think if my father hadn't been killed they would have moved here to live in their retirement. My mother loved sitting out on the deck, listening to the birds. She even tamed a magpie while she was here last.'

'I can see why she loved it so much,' Fran said, looking at the view. 'It's so…so peaceful.'

'I've been doing a bit of work on it here and there. It needed a new kitchen and the floors needed sanding. All I have to do now is paint the spare bedroom and I'm done.'

Fran looked around in awe. Even her do-it-yourself-expert father would have been impressed with the handiwork. The timber floors were smooth and shiny, covered here and there with woven rugs. The open-plan kitchen was decked out in stainless-steel appliances with glass splashbacks along the benches. It led to a dining and family room area that was expansive, the sweeping view of the ocean below making her stop and stare.

'You can see right along the beach from here,' she said. 'It's beautiful.'

He came to stand beside her. 'There's a sea eagle's nest up in those trees over there.'

Fran could feel her senses spring to attention at his closeness. 'Where?' Her voice came out husky and soft.

His shoulder brushed hers as he lifted his arm to point to a scraggly nest at the top of a gumtree. 'There,' he said. 'Can you see that crooked branch up there? It's just to the right of that.'

'I see it…' she said, barely able to breathe.

He dropped his arm back down to his side. 'I often see dolphins and about a month ago a couple of whales cruised past.'

'Wow,' she said, turning to look at him. *Wow is right*, she thought, her heart giving a little stammer as his ice-blue eyes met hers.

She watched as his gaze slipped to her mouth, lingering there for a pulsing moment before moving back to mesh with hers.

She could hear a clock ticking somewhere. It seemed to be measuring the silence, making each second swell with sensual promise.

'Um…your cheek has opened up again,' she said in a husky voice. 'I meant to tell you earlier and I really must see to your arm.'

He put a hand up to his face and grimaced when it came away streaked with blood. 'Maybe I should have got you to dress it for me the first time,' he said with a rueful half-smile.

'I could do it now…I mean, if you would like me to. I mean, if you've got a first-aid kit…or something…' Fran knew she was prattling on like a gauche schoolgirl but she couldn't seem to stop it.

His eyes contained a hint of amusement. 'Come on,' he said. 'The main bathroom is through here. I have a first-aid kit in there.'

Fran concentrated on washing her hands and assembling the things she needed to dress Jacob's arm rather than meet his gaze in the mirror. The bathroom was spacious, with a Balinese theme that was pure luxury, but she felt like she was working from inside a shoebox with Jacob sitting so close on a bath-stool.

'This might sting a bit,' she said as she bathed his burn with antiseptic, carefully wiping away some debris from the wound.

'You have a very gentle touch,' he said. 'I can barely feel a thing.'

Fran had attended to numerous burn patients during her years in A and E but never had one had such an overwhelming effect on her. Her senses were on overload, her nostrils flaring at his male scent, the skin on her face feeling tingly when his breath caressed her as he spoke. She had to work hard to concentrate on what she was doing, instead of staring into those dark-rimmed eyes of his that seemed determined to search for hers whenever he could.

Once the dressing was in place, she put the used items in the bin near the basins. 'Let's have a look at that cheek of yours,' she said, wishing she felt more like a doctor and less like a woman in danger of falling in love.

He held his head at an angle for her to inspect the wound. 'Will I be scarred for life?' he asked.

Fran's hand trembled as she dabbed some Betadine on the wound. 'Not noticeably so,' she said. 'I thought you were going to get a black eye, but apart from a little swelling you've not done too badly.'

'Yeah, I'm pretty tough,' he said as he rose to his feet, his tall figure towering over her. 'You've got to be to get on in communities like this.'

She stepped back and tried to get her breathing to settle back down. 'Your arm…well, vitamin E cream daily will help reduce scarring but you don't strike me as the type to bother with such things.'

He gave her that hint of a smile again. 'If you'd like to freshen up, there's another bathroom down the hall. I'll meet you in a few minutes in the kitchen.'

* * *

Fran made her way to the bathroom, glad of a chance to restore some sort of order to her appearance and her wayward emotions. She washed her hands and face and quickly finger-combed her hair, trying not to be too harsh on her windblown reflection.

When she came out Jacob was in the kitchen with Rufus. Jacob had changed his shorts and flung on a white cotton shirt, buttoned to about halfway up his chest, giving her an eyeful of muscle-bound flesh and masculine hair that her fingers itched to trail through.

He had given the dog a huge bowl of water, which was now half-empty. Rufus was lying on the cool floorboards, totally relaxed as if he lived there.

'Nice for some,' Jacob said, nodding towards the dog.

Fran felt a smile tug at her mouth. 'You're really good with him. Have you ever had a dog of your own?'

'Yes, when I was a kid. I would have one now but I work so many shifts it wouldn't be fair on the dog. When the time is right I will, though.'

Fran wondered what he meant by the right time. Was he thinking of settling down with someone, perhaps having a family? She wanted to ask but thought it was a bit forward. She barely knew him.

'Would you like a cold drink or tea or coffee?' Jacob asked.

'I know this probably sounds stupid on a warm day like this but I would really like a cup of tea,' she said.

'It doesn't sound stupid to me.' He reached for the kettle and filled it under the tap. 'Why don't you head out to the deck and take in the view while I get it ready?'

Fran went through the sliding doors and sat on one of the cushioned lounges, breathing in the breeze that carried a hint of the salty sea with it. A flock of sulphur-crested cockatoos was screeching as they jostled for position on the branches of the gumtree about halfway down the path. The sun was low in the sky, throwing pastel hues over the horizon, soft pink, mauve and a hint of washed-out orange in the cloudless sky, signalling another fine warm day ahead.

The hectic pace of Melbourne suddenly seemed a long way away. Before the night of her attack Fran had not really noticed how busy the city was, or how rushed everyone seemed to be. She had been a part of it, caught up in the race of getting things done, juggling work and the occasional attempt at a social life, feeling satisfied as each week closed that she had achieved everything she had set out to achieve.

Then three minutes had changed everything.

And she couldn't—no matter how hard she tried—change it back.

Jacob carried a tray with two cups and a pot of tea out to the deck. Fran was sitting looking at the view with a wistful expression on her face. With her long blonde hair and clear skin with no hint of make-up she looked about sixteen. She had a coltish figure, slim and leggy but still very feminine, and she had a soft mouth—that was one of the first things he had noticed about her but it was nearly always turned downwards, as if she found smiling uncomfortable.

'Here we go,' he said, setting the tray down on the outdoor coffee table next to her seat. 'Help yourself. There's milk and sugar if you take it and those cookies are some of Beryl Hadley's. She's taken me on as a sort of project, I think.'

A quizzical look came into her eyes. 'Oh, really?'

He gave a wry twist of his mouth as he sat on the seat at the other side of the table. 'Yeah, Beryl is one of those women who think every man over thirty should be married with a couple of kids. She's on a mission to find me a suitable wife.'

He watched as two circles of rosy colour pooled in her cheeks as she cradled her cup in both hands. 'I am sure you are quite capable of finding your own partner,' she said with her gaze averted.

'Not so easy down here,' he said as he sat back. He crossed his legs at the ankles and took a sip of his tea. 'But then again I'm in no hurry.'

The lull in conversation made the sound of the cockatoos all the more ear-piercing.

Fran took another sip of the refreshing tea before she spoke. 'So what made you accept the posting down here? Was it just because your mother liked it here?'

He leaned forward to take a cookie from the plate. 'A combination of things, I guess. I wanted a change. Fighting crime in the city can make you pretty cynical after a while. Down here it's different. Of course, people still break the law, but the focus is on helping people in smaller communities like this. You feel you can really make a difference.'

'How long do you intend on staying, or is that up to the powers that be?'

He considered his response for a moment. 'I have some things I would like to achieve while I'm here. So I haven't put a time limit on it. I'm pretty much taking things as they come. I'm still sorting out some of my mother's stuff both here and in Sydney. I don't want to rush into any decision until I feel it's time.'

She looked back at the cup in her hands and took another sip, her gaze going back to the rolling ocean. 'I know this sounds kind of weird but I feel like I would have really liked your mother if I'd met her,' she said. She swung her gaze back to his. 'This is exactly the sort of place I love. It's so peaceful you can hear yourself breathing.'

'Apart from the cockatoos.'

'Yes, I guess you're right.'

Another silence.

'More tea?' he asked.

Fran shook her head. 'No, that was lovely, thank you.' She put her cup down and, using the wooden arms of the seat, pushed herself upright. 'I guess I should get going. It will be dark soon.'

He rose and gathered the cups back on the tray. 'I'll drive you and Rufus back.'

'You don't have to do that. We can go along the road.'

'I'm going that way anyway,' he said, leading the way back inside. 'Besides, you don't want to be late for your busy evening,' he added over his shoulder.

Fran looked at him in confusion when he turned to face her once he put the tray on the bench. 'I'm not busy. I'm just going home to feed Rufus and watch TV.'

His top lip lifted along with one dark eyebrow. 'So you blew me off for a soap opera, huh?'

Fran felt her cheeks burning, but regardless she jutted her chin. 'I'm not in the habit of accepting dates from men who feel sorry for me.'

'You think that's what it was about?' he asked.

Her lips suddenly felt as dry as charcoal as he locked gazes with her. She sent the tip of her tongue out to moisten her mouth, her belly flip-flopping when he stepped closer. 'W-what are you doing?' she asked, surprised her voice came out at all, let alone as scratchy as it did.

'What do you think I'm doing?' he asked, still holding her gaze.

Fran flattened the middle of her spine against the bench, her heart feeling as if it was going to break through her ribcage. 'Um…I'm not sure…'

His eyes still contained that spark of amusement, or was it mockery? She couldn't quite tell. She held her breath as he reached past her waist, his arm brushing her there, setting off fireworks underneath her skin. Every pore came alive, dancing, leaping and exploding with excitement. She ran her tongue over her lips, wondering if he was going to kiss her. The atmosphere suddenly seemed charged with the possibility. Her heart rate picked up, her spine tingled, her belly quivered, her eyelashes fluttered once or twice, her eyes flicking to his mouth so close…so close…

Then she heard the rattle of his keys as he brought his arm back to his side. 'My keys were on the bench,' he said, dangling them from his fingers.

Fran blinked. 'Oh…right…of course…' She let out her breath in stages, her cheeks feeling furnace-hot as his eyes continued to hold hers.

He smiled that half-smile again. 'Not that I wasn't thinking about doing what you were thinking I was going to do,' he said, his eyes flicking to her mouth and back again.

Her eyes widened but she tried to keep her voice airy and light. 'You think you can read my mind, Sergeant Hawke?'

He lifted his hand and outlined her mouth with the pad of his index finger, taking his time, lingering over the sensitive labrum of her top lip until every nerve was sensitised. Fran quivered under his touch, her breath stalling, her spine feeling as if a stream of warmed honey instead of muscles and ligaments was trying to keep her vertebrae in place. Her heart tap-danced in her chest, a crazy dance that made her feel dizzy.

'I guess since you were expecting me to kiss you, maybe

I ought to go right ahead and do it,' he said, brushing her bottom lip with the pad of his thumb.

Somehow Fran got her voice to work; she even got it to sound tart, even a little sarcastic. 'Please don't feel at all obligated.'

Her breath caught in her throat as he stepped closer. She could feel his hips within touching distance, and at one point he brushed against her, the intimate contact of his very male body making every sense of hers switch to overload.

The tension in the air was almost palpable. She felt every second humming with it.

Fran dared not look at his mouth. She wanted to but knew if she did she would not be able to resist closing the distance and pressing hers to his to see if it was as warm and sensual and commanding as it looked. She kept her eyes on his, even though she could feel herself drowning in their startling blue depths.

'I'm not sure it would be a good idea for you to…for me to…for us to…you know…get involved…' She faltered.

He held her gaze for a throbbing beat or two before stepping back from her. 'Pity,' he said in an offhand tone. 'But let me know if you change your mind.'

Fran frowned at his casual, laid-back manner. Her heart was still hammering like a piston while he seemed largely unaffected. She didn't know whether to be insulted or disappointed, although she knew if she was honest with herself, she was both. Was he on the hunt for a temporary playmate and thought she would fit the position? How demeaning! But then again she *had* wanted him to kiss her.

The let-down, out-of-sorts feeling lingering in her stomach was annoying. She wondered if he had been playing with her, testing her to see what sort of woman she was. She knew there were plenty of her peers who would think nothing of a casual fling with an attractive partner. One-night stands or having a sex buddy was commonplace these days. But she wasn't built that way.

'Rufus, time to go home,' she said briskly, slapping her hands against her thighs to get the dog's attention.

Rufus got up from the floor and came over with his tail wagging and sat at Jacob's feet, looking up at him adoringly.

Fran felt like rolling her eyes. She folded her arms and tilted her head at the dog admonishingly. 'Traitor.'

Jacob ruffled Rufus's ears and jangled his keys. 'Ever been in a police car before, Dr Nin?' he asked.

She squared her shoulders and sent him a brittle look. 'No.'

He held open the front door for her, amused by her stiff carriage. 'Loosen up, sweetheart,' he said. 'You're not under arrest.'

Her eyes widened momentarily at the endearment, but just as quickly she lowered her gaze, her small white teeth sinking into her bottom lip as she brushed past him to make her way to the car.

Jacob moved ahead to open the car door for her, noting how her limp had worsened. She caught the tail end of his empathetic look and immediately set her mouth, a mantle of cold hauteur coming over her as she got into the passenger seat.

He waited until Rufus was stowed safely in the back and he was behind the wheel before he spoke. 'I have a home gym with some equipment that might help strengthen your leg. I broke mine a few years back in a car chase. I could write out a programme for you. You'd be amazed at the way it helps.'

Her eyes met his for a brief moment before turning to stare sightlessly out of the windscreen. 'I'll think about it,' she said in a small stiff voice.

Jacob pulled down his seat belt and clicked it into place. 'You do that,' he said, and, gunning the engine, drove out of his property, leaving a spray of gravel in his wake.

CHAPTER SIX

THE drive back to her sister's house took only a few minutes but just as Jacob was pulling into the drive his radio informed him of a hit-and-run accident just out of town.

'I've got Dr Nin with me right now,' Jacob said to Constable Jeffrey. He glanced at Fran. 'Have you still got the trauma kit from Candi Broderick's fall?'

'It's at my sister's place,' Fran said, feeling her nerves tighten beneath her skin like steel wires under extreme pressure.

Not a hit and run. Not a roadside rescue with no back-up. She couldn't do it. She would have to tell him. Right now. She would have to come straight out and tell him what a coward she was, what a failure, what a nervous wreck....

'We're about ten minutes away,' Jacob said to the constable on the radio. 'How far away are the ambos?'

Fran heard the constable's voice crackle over the radio. 'Two volunteers are on their way. They should be almost there by now.'

Jacob was out of the car and opening her door before she had unclipped her seat belt. She forced her stiff leg to move and hurried inside to collect the kit, pushing Rufus inside as she went.

When she got back in the police vehicle she sucked in a breath as Jacob put his foot to the floor. He turned on the lights and siren, the sense of urgency making her blood pound.

Keep calm, keep calm, keep calm, she chanted to herself, mantra-like.

The car's speed pushed her back in her seat but she kept working on keeping herself focussed and in control. She'd done roadside retrievals with mock patients during trauma training a few years ago. She had dealt with hundreds of cases of trauma in A and E but that had been with help and every medical aid you could ask for. Treating a real patient at a dusty roadside was going to test her in every way imaginable. The ambulance officers were volunteers, not trained paramedics. Small communities like Pelican Bay could not afford a full-time service. Fran knew she would be expected to take charge as she had with Candi and Ella, and the thought of the unknown terrified her. How badly would the victim be injured? Hit-and-run accidents could be anything from a slight clip with barely any damage to a victim being crushed, dragged or thrown by the vehicle. Various scenarios flashed through her brain, each one ramping up her panic. She was out of her depth. She was not as experienced as she should be for a situation like this. She was still getting over her own trauma—how could she possibly manage someone else's? What if she had another blank moment like she'd had with little Ella? Jacob was a competent cop but she doubted he would be able to take over if she fell apart.

She clenched her hands into tight fists in her lap, using every second of the journey to try and mentally prepare herself for who knew what.

As Jacob drove along the Rainbow Creek Road, about fifteen kilometres out of the Bay, Fran could see the ambulance had already arrived. The two volunteers looked up from the patient with visible relief, one of them hurrying towards her as she got out of the car.

'We've got a serious head injury and a leg fracture,' the woman in her sixties said. 'He's barely breathing. Mick's trying to give him some oxygen now.'

Fran took a steadying breath and, approaching the victim, quickly assessed the situation. The man was about fifty, one of his thighs at an acute angle, dark blood seeping onto the road from a head injury. And as the volunteer had said, he was hardly breathing.

'Can you get me a cervical collar?' she asked the woman who had introduced herself as Karen.

Once she had the collar on, Fran asked for the portable sucker to be set up. She quickly donned gloves and goggles and suggested Jacob do the same. He was looking down at the victim, his expression inscrutable.

'Sergeant Hawke?' she prompted, frowning at him.

He appeared to give himself a mental shake. 'Sorry?'

'You'd better glove up,' she repeated. 'And goggles, too, in case there are blood splashes. You also, Karen, and Mick, is it?'

'Yeah.' The man nodded.

Fran used the sucker on the victim's mouth before she inserted a Guedel's airway and administered oxygen. There was no response from the victim to voice or pain. Although the airway was clear, he had stopped breathing.

'Can you pull on his leg to straighten it?' she asked Mick, and once he had done so, with Jacob and Karen's help they log-rolled the man onto the spinal board while Fran controlled the neck.

As soon as Fran had the patient on his back she could see

the front of the neck had been in an impact with whatever had hit him and that the larynx was probably crushed, which meant the likelihood of intubating would be remote.

'I'm going to have to put in a surgical airway,' she said, reaching for a disposable scalpel, forcing her hand to stay steady and controlled while inside she felt doubt nip at her nerves with sharp pointed teeth as she made the incision.

'Mick, you ventilate him while I listen to his chest,' she directed.

'Er…this is my first time,' Mick said, a fire-engine blush running over his cheeks. 'I'm not sure I can do it properly.'

Fran swung her gaze to the female officer. 'Karen?'

'Sergeant Hawke had better do it,' Karen said with a grimace. 'Mick and I are not very experienced. Jack's on leave this week and Hamish is out of town. We were the only two available.'

'Right, Sergeant,' Fran said, but before she could instruct him on what to do he had already taken over with the sort of competence she had come to expect from him. His cool, calm composure helped her. It suddenly occurred to her how automatic her responses to the scene had been so far. It helped her shattered confidence somewhat, good enough to keep going for now.

'OK…' She took another deep breath and, reaching for a stethoscope, addressed Karen. 'Can you cut the patient's shirt off his chest?'

Karen did as she was directed and Fran leant down to listen to the man's chest. There was no air on entry to the right side. All the signs pointed to a tension pneumonthorax, which was rapidly fatal if not treated immediately.

Before early management of severe trauma courses had been conducted in Australia, giving doctors the skills to recognise and deal with injuries such as this, many patients had died because of the failure of those attending them to prioritise their assessment and treatment. ABCDE—airway, breathing, circulation, disability, exposure/environment—and treat each injury as it was found.

Fran mentally rehearsed the stages of primary survey as she located a large-bore IV needle. After wiping it with an alcohol swab, she inserted the needle a few millimetres at a time over the top border of the third rib and into the second intercostal space on the right, sensing a 'pop' as the needle punctured the pleura. There was an immediate hiss of air out of the needle. Quickly glancing at Jacob, Fran could see the ventilation of the victim had become easier.

'So far so good,' she said, more to herself than to the others, thrilled that she had got this far without falling apart.

'You certainly know what you're doing,' Karen remarked. 'Thank God you're in town right now, otherwise this guy wouldn't have a chance.'

Fran acknowledged Karen's comment with a strained smile, although deep inside she felt another link of confidence snap into place as she inserted a canula into a large vein in each of the patient's arms, rapidly infusing normal saline.

'Mick, can you take his pulse and BP?' she asked, glancing up as another police car with two officers arrived, one of them the young officer she had met before, Constable Jeffrey.

Mick nodded. 'Yep, onto it now.'

'Karen, if you can use those scissors on his jeans now, please,' Fran said. 'I need to check that foot pulse and get a blow-up splint on.'

'Pulse is 140 and BP 80 over 50,' Mick informed her.

Once the splint was in place, Fran carefully examined the head wound. There was no bony fracture underlying the laceration but she noted the unequal pupils as she lifted each eyelid. She bandaged the bleeding scalp wound and once she had the patient as stable as she could, she supervised his loading into the ambulance with the assistance of the two police officers who had just arrived.

One of them had called for helicopter evacuation at Jacob's command and informed Fran it would be landing on the cricket oval near the clinic within the next half-hour.

Jacob had handed over the ventilation to Karen, who seemed more confident once she had been shown how to do it. He moved around the accident site, crouching down at one point to inspect the gravel, Fran supposed for skid or swerve marks. He still had that inscrutable expression on his face, but she could sense something in his stance that made her wonder what was going on behind the screen of those ice-blue eyes of his.

He caught her looking at him and, stripping off his blood-stained gloves, put them in the bin in the back of the ambulance. 'Whoever hit him did a good job of it,' he said. 'If you hadn't been on hand he wouldn't have lasted long enough to get him in the chopper.'

Fran felt her cheeks begin to glow at his compliment. From the moment she had met him he hadn't struck her as the type to throw words around just to people-please. What he said, when he said it, was genuine. 'How could someone run into another person and just drive off like that?' she asked.

He looked back at the victim lying on the stretcher for a moment. He turned back to meet her frowning gaze. 'It takes all types, Dr Nin.' He let out a sigh that seemed to be somewhere between resignation at the state of the world and relief that he was no longer needed as roadside assistant. 'It takes all types.'

After loading the patient into the ambulance, Fran inserted an intercostal chest drain to better manage the pneumothorax, and on the way to the clinic she catheterised the patient and inserted a nasogastric tube. By the time they arrived, she had completed her secondary survey, noting several additional injuries. The patient was still deeply unconscious but his blood pressure was nearly back to normal.

She communicated by mobile phone to the receiving hospital, giving them a rundown of the patient's injuries and how she had managed them to this point. The words rolled off her tongue as they had done so many times in the past, and she wondered if this was another limping step forward on the long, twisting road to recovery.

The blades of the helicopter created a wind that lifted Fran's hair about her face as the victim was finally loaded. The Careflight team was trauma trained and took over the management of the patient, congratulating her for the job she had done.

Fran brushed her hair back off her face and stood watching as the helicopter lifted off, hoping the man made it in spite of his life-threatening injuries.

Constable Jeffrey came over to where she was standing. 'Sergeant Hawke instructed me to give you a lift home,' he said.

Fran glanced around. 'Where is he? I thought he followed the ambulance back to town.'

'He's back at the accident site,' he said. 'I've got to go back there once I take you home to do further investigations.'

'Do you know who the victim is?' she asked as Constable Jeffrey drove to her sister's house.

'He didn't have any ID on him but apparently he's a fairly new resident to the bay. Wade Smith's his name, or so

Sergeant Hawke said. Comes from Sydney originally—he knew him back there.'

Fran lifted her brows as she glanced at him. 'In a personal or professional sense?'

Constable Jeffrey gave her a mask-like look which reminded her of every cop she had ever met, in particular Jacob Hawke. 'He's got a record, if that's what you mean. Car theft, aggravated assault, domestic violence, you name it, he's been there and done it. He's supposed to be on the straight and narrow now but how long that will last is anyone's guess.'

Fran chewed her lip. Patients were patients, no matter what they did or who they were. She would not have treated Mr Smith any differently if she had known he was a well-known criminal. As far as she was concerned, he was a fellow human being who had needed her expertise. But thinking back to those first few minutes at the scene of the accident, she recalled Jacob Hawke's silent scrutiny of the victim.

'Does Mr Smith have family that need to be contacted?' she asked.

'Our people will deal with that,' he said as he parked in the driveway, with the engine still running. 'Thanks for helping out this evening, Dr Nin.'

'No problem,' she said, and got out of the car. She gave him a wave as he drove off, her smile fading as soon as he'd disappeared from sight.

She was tired, filthy and more than a little annoyed that Jacob was occupying her thoughts far more than she wanted him to.

Fran had showered and was just thinking about whether to eat something or not when Rufus pricked up his ears as a car came up the driveway. She pulled the edges of her wrap tighter around her waist, releasing her hair from the neck of it as she went to the door.

Jacob too had showered and changed. He was dressed in blue denim jeans and a white T-shirt, the close-fitting fabric clinging to his muscular form. Every muscle was highlighted, making her want to run her hands over him and feel their taut perfection under her fingertips.

'Sorry to bother you so late,' he said, his gaze swiftly but thoroughly taking in her attire.

'It's fine,' Fran said, opening the door for him to come in, holding the edges of her wrap with the other hand. 'I'm not on my way to bed. I was actually trying to decide whether to have dinner or to give it a miss.'

'You've had a tough day, you should eat something.'

'What about you?' she asked. 'Have you had dinner?'

'I had a lukewarm cup of coffee about an hour ago.'

Fran tucked a damp strand of hair behind her ear. 'I could rustle up something for us both...I mean, if you don't mind... It won't be fancy but...'

'That would be great,' he said with a hint of a smile.

She took a steadying breath and led the way to the kitchen, conscious of him a couple of steps behind. 'Would you like a glass of wine or a beer or something?' she asked as she rummaged in the fridge for ingredients. 'Nick has light beer here if you'd prefer it.'

'Light beer would be perfect,' he said, pulling out one of the kitchen stools. 'I'm off duty now but I don't like to indulge too much in case there's an emergency.'

Fran handed him a bottle of beer before pouring herself a glass of white wine from the bottle that had been open for a couple of days. 'How did Mr Smith's family take the news of his accident?' she asked as she began cracking eggs for an omelette.

'He doesn't have any family down here,' he said. 'He has a brother somewhere, in Wagga, I think.'

She looked up from cracking the third egg. 'So you know him?'

Something shifted in his gaze. 'Not personally.'

She broke another egg and picked up the whisk, her teeth sinking into her bottom lip for a moment. 'I've been thinking about his injuries…'

'Oh?'

She met his gaze across the counter. 'The trauma to his throat was pretty unusual for a hit and run. The broken leg is standard, but the neck…' She lowered her eyes and began to whisk the eggs. 'I don't know…'

'You don't think it was a hit and run?' he asked.

She glanced back at him. 'What do you think?'

He held her look for a beat or two. 'There were no skid marks to indicate a car trying to avoid a collision,' he said. 'There were tyre marks, though, where a car had appeared to stop and taken off again at speed.'

Fran gnawed at her lip again. 'So you think there's a possibility he had been injured somewhere else and dumped there to make it look like a hit and run?'

He ran the pad of his thumb over the lip of his beer bottle, the set to his mouth grim. 'Looks like it.'

She let out a breath without realising she had been holding it. 'Do you have any idea of what sort of motive someone would have for doing such a thing?' she asked. 'Does Mr Smith have enemies down here?'

His expression turned cynical. 'People like Wade Smith have enemies everywhere—they'd follow him like a bad smell.'

'Who reported the accident?' she asked as she put the omelette on the cooktop.

'It was an anonymous call from a mobile phone. We should have the information on who it was by tomorrow.'

'Do you think it was the same person responsible for the accident?' she asked with a frown.

'Not likely,' he said. 'Why would someone who wanted him dead call for help? It's more likely a local found him and didn't want to get involved, called it in once they'd left the scene. There were other tyre tracks—it's a matter of working out which ones belong to which vehicles.'

Fran picked up her wine, unable to suppress a faint shiver. 'It creeps me out to think of someone wandering around town who would think nothing of maiming someone so severely.'

'Do you think he will survive?'

'I think so, his body anyway,' she said, turning to check on the omelette. 'But the brain injury…that could be severe or maybe he'll just wake up with a headache and amnesia for the whole episode. We'll know after he comes off the ventilator.'

Jacob drummed two of his fingers on the side of his beer bottle. 'You did a fantastic job out there, Dr Nin. That was a tough call but you handled it brilliantly. I have to confess I had my doubts about you before, but you took control as if on autopilot or something.'

She met his eyes again, twisting her mouth ruefully. 'Can we quit the Doctor and Sergeant routine?'

'Sure,' he said, smiling that half-smile. 'Fran, then.'

'Thanks,' she said. 'But I have to tell you I was terrified out there.'

'You didn't show it.'

She bit her lip. 'I can see how this place really needs a full-time doctor.'

'Are you reconsidering taking it on?' he asked. 'Linda told me she has a clinic already fully booked for Friday.'

Fran picked up her wine again, twirling the glass rather than drinking from it. 'I know,' she said. 'I got her message on my voicemail. But I'm an emergency medicine physician. I spent years training to be the best I could be, but…' Her teeth savaged her lip again. 'I'm not a GP.'

'It seems to me cops are a little like doctors,' he said. 'We have to keep fairly general in our knowledge and experience. I've worked in traffic and the drug squad and even a stint in covert operations, but a cop is a cop, much the same as a doctor is a doctor. The training is almost hardwired into us. It seemed like that out there today when you took charge as if you'd been doing it every day of your life.'

Fran's hand trembled as she put down her wineglass. She frowned as she dished up the omelette, wondering where to begin, wondering why she wanted to tell him when she had refused to talk about it with anyone else. Maybe it was because she felt he would understand. After all, he had suffered because of what a criminal had done to his father. He carried that pain; she saw it in him, the way he held part of himself back, the way he rationed his smiles.

She handed him a plate with a large serving of salad and fluffy cheese omelette on it before she sat on the stool opposite, with some food for herself. 'Jacob, there's something you should know about me…'

His eyes centred on hers, not a muscle on his face moving as he silently watched her.

Fran moistened her lips and began again, 'I know you think I'm a city chick with an attitude problem, and to some degree I've encouraged that view. It was easier than offering an explanation for my behaviour just about every time we've met up.'

Still he remained silent.

Fran looked down at her plate, shifting her food for a moment before returning her gaze to his unwavering one. 'It was a busy Friday night,' she said. 'I've had hundreds of them during my career. There were patients lined up on trolleys and chairs, waiting for beds on the wards. I guess you know how rundown the public health-care system is. Security had been called to deal with a drunk who was shouting abuse at the staff. I was called to deal with a new admission, another young man who had come in with lacerations to both his arms…' She stopped and swallowed.

'Go on,' Jacob said in a low deep tone.

She looked at him, her voice sounding hollow as she continued. 'It was like someone had turned a switch on him somewhere. He was agitated when he came in certainly, but I thought that was because of his injury. But suddenly he became uncontrollably violent. He threw me up against the wall. I screamed for help but he slammed his fist into my face. I think I might have lost consciousness briefly but I came to and found him stomping on my leg. The pain…' She grimaced and went on, 'I tried to get away but he hauled me up again and the last thing I remember is his fist coming towards me again…'

Jacob felt his insides churn. For all his years as a police officer he still couldn't stomach violence, particularly violence against women and children. He had attended briefings on dealing with drug-fuelled assailants and he had experienced it firsthand in Sydney too many times to count. The level of violence was astonishing. People affected by crystal meth—ice, as it was known on the street—developed bursts of superhuman strength. Once the effects of the drug wore off, most were not even aware of what they had done or the havoc they had caused. Even excess alcohol had a similar effect on some people, and that was a problem that was worsening with binge drinking.

It was no wonder Fran was questioning her career choice. Who wouldn't think twice about returning to the fray to perhaps face the same again? He had seen plenty of cops give the job away for less. Little Frances Nin was a very courageous young woman for stepping into the breach as she had so far while she had been in the Bay. How she had done it, given what she had been through, amazed him.

'I was in a coma for three weeks,' she said into the silence. 'No one was sure whether I was going to be the same person when or if I woke up.' She gave him a rueful look. 'And I guess I'm not the same person.'

Jacob cleared his throat. 'No one could be the same after such an experience,' he said, his voice coming out sounding rusty. 'You've done well to get this far.'

She gave him another rueful grimace. 'Apart from my leg.'

'I could help you with that,' he said. 'I meant what I said earlier today. You can use my gym any time.'

She toyed with the stem of her glass, her mouth pulled down at the corners. 'He left me because of it,' she said after a moment. 'The guy I was seeing. Not that it was serious or anything—we were just going on the casual date when work allowed—but it became pretty obvious he couldn't handle a damaged partner. He traded me in for a newer, updated model. One who can wear sky-high heels and run like a gazelle.'

Jacob shook his head in disbelief.

She picked up her wineglass and gave it another twirl, tilting her head to one side as she searched his features. 'Maybe I will try out that gym of yours,' she said. 'Maybe it's time I stopped feeling sorry for myself too.'

Jacob put his barely touched meal aside and came around to her side of the counter.

'What are you doing?' she asked, her eyes flaring slightly.

'What I wanted to do earlier this afternoon,' he said, placing his hands on each side of her narrow waist as he drew her to her feet.

She quivered at his touch, her tongue darting out to moisten her lips. 'Oh…'

He hooked one brow upwards. 'Oh?'

She gave him a nervous flicker of a smile. 'I mean *Oh*.'

His gaze dropped to her mouth, her beautiful soft mouth that he had dreamt of kissing for days. His groin tightened, his spine tingled, and, taking a breath that snagged on something deep inside his chest, he lowered his mouth to hers.

CHAPTER SEVEN

FRAN had dreamt of his mouth for days. She had watched him speak with it, she had watched him do that half-smile with it and she had seen him twist it in concentration and even flatten it in anger. But none of that prepared her for how it would feel against hers.

At the very first contact of his lips on hers she felt a rush of sensation go through her that was completely spellbinding. His mouth was firm but there was softness in it too, surprising gentleness that stirred her deeply. Her mouth buzzed beneath the pressure of his, every nerve swelling beneath the surface of her lips to take more of him in.

She felt the slow brush of his tongue against the seam of her mouth, her legs almost collapsing as he gently pushed through to claim her totally. The sexy rasp of his tongue against hers sent her into a sensual vortex. Her spine tingled as he explored the moist cave of her mouth, stroking her tongue, teasing it, cajoling it to join his in a dance that left her breathless with a longing she had never felt to that extent before.

She felt his hands leave her waist to bury themselves in her hair, his fingers splaying against her scalp as he angled her head to deepen the kiss even further. Her heart raced as his tongue stabbed teasingly at hers, mimicking the physical intimacy his body craved. She could feel the swollen length of him against her, his arousal making her feel womanly and attractive, and powerfully feminine in a way she had never felt with anyone else.

She had been kissed many times before; she had even made love many times—well, maybe not *that* many times, she thought a little ruefully. Her first lover had been early in medical school and sex had always been a bit of a rushed affair, always leaving her feeling a bit up in the air, uncompleted, unsatisfied, and nearly always blaming herself.

But somehow this one kiss with Jacob put her senses in a place they had never been previously. It was as if her whole body had come alive for the first time ever. It was throbbing inside and out, aching, pulsing, excited, exhilarated with feelings foreign to her. Her breasts prickled and ached with tension, the tightening of her flesh making her hungry for his touch.

She could almost imagine how his calloused hands would feel on her tender flesh—abrasive, masculine, possessive and totally mind-blowing. Then she thought of his mouth on her, hot, wet, his tongue laving her, his mouth sucking on her until her nipples were engorged and swollen. Her mind hurtled out of control with the erotic images.

'God, I should stop right now,' he groaned just above her lips, his fingers burying deeper into her hair as if anchoring himself. 'For pity's sake, tell me to stop.'

Fran shivered in delight as the breath of his statement danced over the surface of her kiss-swollen lips. Every hair on her head felt sensitised. Her scalp prickled and warmed with excitement, and her breathing became hectic and uneven as she sent her tongue out, tasting him, taking that arrant male taste into her mouth and swallowing it, relishing in it.

'Oh…' was all she could manage.

He gave her a crooked smile. 'Oh?'

She smiled back, but shyly. 'Oh as in oh-h-h.' She let her voice go down in disappointment.

His eyes glittered with desire as he looked back down at her mouth. 'You know, this could become a bit of habit,' he said in a gravel-rough tone that curled her toes. 'Kissing you, I mean.'

Fran shivered again as his hands left her hair and went to the small of her back, bringing her hard up against him. Her stomach quivered at the contact, hard to soft, male to female. 'Oh?' Again it was all she could get past her trembling lips.

'Yes.' His mouth slanted sexily as he brought it back down to hers.

Fran breathed in the scent of him, her eyes closing as he took her on another sensual journey, each thrilling step of the way a total enlightenment to her. How could one pair of lips evoke so much feeling? How could one tongue communicate desire in so many ways? That sexy sweeping action, that gentle stroking and the delicious little thrusts that spilled a fountain of need inside her. She could feel the walls of her inner body melting, the hot liquid of desire pooling between her thighs.

Her arms somehow ended up around his neck, her fingers threading through his thick dark hair, his groan of response delighting her as she kissed him back. Her lips played with his, nibbling at his bottom lip, soft little nips that tugged and tethered simultaneously.

Jacob dragged his mouth off hers. 'O-K,' he said, his breathing more than a little ragged, 'definitely time to stop.'

She gazed up at him, her arms still around his neck, her fingers making tiny caressing circles in his hair. It made the hairs on the back of his neck quiver as they stood upright, and a warm, lava-like feeling pooled at the base of his spine.

God, he wanted her. When was the last time he had felt this level of arousal? He'd had his fair share of sexual partners. Not as many as some of his mates, but he had never been interested in one-night stands. His work had shown him the dangers of casual sex, not just disease and infections but how things could be misinterpreted, how without the context of a relationship the lines could so easily become blurred.

And yet sex had still been a purely physical thing for him. A mutually enjoyable partnership, but somehow this was different. Way different.

He didn't want to stop.

He didn't know how he *had* stopped.

He just knew he didn't want to end this spell that had whipped him into thinking things he was not used to thinking.

'I guess you're right,' she said, dropping her arms from around his neck and taking a small step backwards. Her cheeks were flushed like a pale pink rose, her grey-blue eyes all dark inkspot pupils, her mouth soft and swollen, as if it had been stung.

Jacob brushed his fingertip against the curve of her chin where his skin had grazed her. Seeing the red patch on her creamy skin made something inside his chest give slightly.

'Sorry,' he said heavily. 'I should have shaved before I came around.'

She put a hand to her face, her slim fingers tracing over the spot. 'It's fine…' Her voice was soft, whisper-soft. 'I can't even feel it.'

He drew in a hitching breath and before he could stop himself he leaned down to press a feather-light kiss to the graze.

He lifted his head, but not far enough.

Time stood still for an infinitesimal moment.

He watched as the point of her tongue came out, shyly, tentatively, and deposited a fine sheen of moisture over her blood-red lips. His groin tightened further, his heart rate escalating as he leaned down again. He felt her quickly expelled breath against his lips, a little gasp of surprise and excitement that fuelled his desire like a freshly struck match to bone-dry tinder. He watched as her eyelashes fluttered and slowly closed, and then his mouth came back down and sealed hers.

Fran sighed with pleasure as his lips worked their magic all over again. His hands were on her hips, his fingers splayed against her, holding her to his throbbing heat. She put her arms around his waist, her hands exploring the well-formed muscles of his back, before dipping lower to his taut buttocks. He planted his legs either side of hers, bracketing her body with his. It made her aware of every hard ridge of him, the latent power of him making her heart race as his body pulsed with longing against hers.

He made a sound deep in his throat, a very male, very aroused sound that made her stomach go into freefall. And then his hands moved up from her hips, slowly, tantalisingly slowly, stalling just below the curve of her breasts. She shifted against him, offering herself to him, aching to feel his palms on her, touching her, shaping her, possessing her.

His hands cupped her through her lightweight robe, the flimsy satin not enough to withstand the warmth of his palms. 'Nice,' he rumbled against her lips.

'Mmm…' she breathed back dreamily.

'Should stop now,' he added, trailing one finger down the shadow of her cleavage.

'I guess…' She shivered as his fingertip brushed the inner side of her breast, the sensitive skin bursting with sensation.

'You know…before I do something totally inappropriate,' he went on, parting her robe just a little, his mouth branding the upper curve of her right breast in a scorch of male lips against bare feminine flesh.

'Mmm,' she said, arching her spine.

'You're not helping me here, Fran,' he said in mock reproach as he gave her other breast the same searing kiss.

'I kn-know…' She shivered against him again. 'Crazy, isn't it?'

He peeled the robe back a little further, his thumb rolling over the tight bud of her nipple, making her gasp out loud. 'The trouble is, of course, that practically every time I see you, you're half dressed,' he growled playfully.

Fran gave him a coy smile. 'So you noticed that first day, huh?'

His eyes darkened as they held hers. 'Damn right I did, and that other day on the beach.'

She arched her brows and angled her head as she looked up at him pointedly. 'Which other day?'

His thumb was still caressing her nipple, his eyes locked on hers. 'Every day since you've been in town.'

Her eyes widened. 'You saw me sunbathing?'

He tapped her on the end of her nose. 'I hope you were wearing sunscreen, Dr Nin.'

'Always,' she said, blushing again. 'I just wanted to live a little dangerously for once. My sister sort of egged me on. She said no one would see me.'

He smiled that sexy smile once more. 'Don't worry, I didn't see too much. I was too far away.'

'I hope you're not obliquely inferring I am too small in that department,' Fran said with a little frown of insecurity pulling at her brow.

'Of course not,' he said, frowning back. 'You're beautiful. Perfect, in fact.'

She bit her lower lip. 'Sorry for being so sensitive…it's just it was a bit of an issue with one of my ex-boyfriends. He seemed to think I would benefit from some enhancement. He even offered to refer me to a colleague of his.'

'What a jerk,' Jacob muttered darkly.

Fran felt her smile come from inside her chest; it bloomed and bloomed until it burst out on her lips. 'You know something, Sergeant Hawke? You're a really nice man.'

He gave her a rueful look and pulled the edges of her robe together. 'Thanks for reminding me.'

Her shoulders went down. 'Oh…'

He pressed a brief, hard kiss to her mouth. 'Come to my place on Friday late afternoon,' he said. 'I'll show you how to use my equipment in the gym.'

'I don't want to impose…'

He tucked a strand of her hair behind her ear, the gentle touch of his fingers sending another river of sensation cascading down her spine. 'Afterwards I'll make us some dinner,' he said. 'Nothing special, so don't get your hopes up.'

Fran gave him a smile. 'I'm sure it will be lovely. Would you like me to bring something?'

'No, just come about five-thirty or so,' he said. 'Or would you like me to pick you up?'

Fran suddenly frowned. 'I'm not sure what to do about the clinic…'

'The clinic Linda rescheduled for tomorrow?'

She nodded and lowered her eyes. 'I didn't have a headache today, which I think you already know…'

He tipped up her chin with his finger. 'Want to tell me what happened?'

She chewed at her lip. 'I was all set to go in…well I was parked out in front at least…'

'And?'

She swallowed tightly. 'I started to walk up the path when I heard the sirens—I guess it was you on your way to the fire. The fire engine was on your tail and all the noise…it just got to me. I panicked, *really* panicked. I thought I was going to pass out.'

'You poor kid,' he said gently.

'Linda came out and found me looking like a total zombie,' she said. 'How could I explain it all to her? I felt such a fool. All I could think was I had to get out of there, and fast. I told her the first thing that came to mind, which was sort of true as by the time I got back to Caro's place my head was pounding.'

Jacob put his hands on her shoulders. 'Have you had panic attacks before?'

'Yes…' Her cheeks went bright red. 'I haven't told anyone but you, not even my sister. Everyone expects doctors to be able to cope with anything. We see blood and death and serious injury all the time, but I just can't seem to walk into a hospital without breaking out in a cold sweat.' She looked up at him. 'You should have seen me trying to get through the doors of Wollongong Hospital to visit Caro and the babies. It took me twenty attempts before I could summon up the courage.'

Jacob cupped the nape of her neck as he held her gaze. 'I'm

sorry for bullying you practically non-stop about taking up the position at the clinic. I wish I had known. I wish your sister or Nick had mentioned something to me. Why didn't they?'

'Because I swore them to secrecy,' she confessed with a sheepish look. 'I know it probably sounds silly but I want to deal with it in my own time. People treat me differently when they find out what happened. I hate being pitied. I just want to find my own way through this, however long it takes.'

'Fran, I've had colleagues lose it completely over things they've seen or been through,' he said. 'Some make it back, others don't. But the one thing you must focus on is trying to get your life back. You are a talented doctor. It would be a shame to see that talent go to waste.'

Fran stepped out of his hold. 'Ever since I was eight I have wanted to be an A and E specialist. I fell off my bike and broke my arm and the experience of the caring doctors left a huge impression on me. I have never thought of being anything but an emergency specialist. I just don't see myself as a country GP.'

'Did I say you had to commit to being a GP?' he asked. 'I'm just suggesting it might be a way to ease yourself back into things, to rebuild your confidence.'

Fran let out a breath. 'I'm not making any promises, Jacob. I can't, can't you see that?'

He stepped back and took her by the shoulders again. 'What if I come with you the first couple of times? Would that help?'

She looked up at him in wonder. 'You would do that?'

'I'm a cop, Fran,' he said. 'I'm meant to protect the public, which includes you.'

She gnawed at her bottom lip again. 'I guess I can't pretend I've got another headache.'

'No, that probably won't go down too well.'

'But what will people think of you being there like some sort of bodyguard?' she asked.

'I'll try not to make it too obvious,' he said. 'I can come and go depending on how you are coping. You can even check my burn for me.'

Fran still felt doubtful but incredibly grateful for his support. She felt as if a burdensome weight had been taken off her shoulders just by telling him what had happened. It made her feelings towards him a little harder to ignore. 'I hate being such a bother,' she said. 'I am sure you have much better things to do with your time than hold my hand while I find my feet, if indeed I ever do.'

Jacob picked up her hand and pressed a kiss to the middle of her palm. 'Just take things a step at a time, Fran. No one is asking you to commit to anything. Just go with the flow to see how things work out. You're here, you're available and the town needs you. No one is making you commit for life. It's just for now. Enjoy it for what it is.'

Fran nodded in acquiescence, but after he left a minute or two later she wondered if he had been referring not just to the clinic but to their relationship.

Relationship? she chided herself as she cleaned up the dishes from their meal. What relationship? All he had done was kiss her. Sure, he'd asked her for a meal the following evening, but it was far too early to be thinking in terms of whether he intended taking things further, as in regularly dating her.

She loaded the dishwasher, her brow furrowed as she thought about the future. Even if she did date him, she wasn't planning on staying in Pelican Bay longer than three months. Once the babies were home and in a routine Caro and Nick would need to get on with their lives without her intruding on their new family dynamics.

Of course, she could find a little place by the sea; she had some money saved up, the victim compensation she had received from the court case would certainly leave her more or less debt free. Besides, her sister had made the change without a hiccup. But, then, Caro had fallen in love with Nick Atkins and would have followed him anywhere.

Fran blew out a sigh as she closed the dishwasher. Was *she* falling in love? Just thinking about what had happened between Jacob and her earlier made her chest felt fluttery, as if a moth was trapped inside her chest. Her heart felt tight, as if a hand was squeezing it. And her stomach felt nervous and excited at the same time at the thought of spending tomorrow evening with him.

Just the two of them.

Alone.

CHAPTER EIGHT

AS THEY had arranged the evening before, Jacob met Fran outside the clinic on Friday morning. He got off his police bike, lifting the visor of his helmet to smile at her with his eyes. 'Hi.'

'Hi,' she said shyly, nervously twisting her sweaty hands together.

'How are you feeling?' he asked as he removed his helmet and placed it under his arm.

'OK, I guess,' Fran said. 'It's funny but since we had that talk last night I've felt a lot better about things...you know, the incident. It was the first time in ages I didn't have a nightmare.'

He briefly captured her hand and gave it a gentle squeeze. 'That's great progress, Fran. You're a brave young woman.'

Fran glowed under his praise and barely noticed the steps they took towards the clinic entrance.

Linda looked up from the reception counter and immediately apologised for the crowd in the waiting room. 'How's your head, Dr Nin?' she added before Fran could even respond to her apology. 'I told the last five patients who came in that the whole day was already double booked, but do you think they would listen? They insisted, no, *demanded* to see you. I can turn them away if you don't think you can handle it.' Linda glanced past Fran to see Jacob standing there. 'Sergeant? Don't tell me you want an appointment as well?'

Jacob smiled. 'No, thanks, Linda, I'm in robust health. I'm just here to help Dr Nin get settled in. How about I show her through the clinic while you keep control of that phone?'

Linda snorted and rolled her eyes as the phone rang yet again. 'Good idea,' she said. Picking up the phone, she answered, 'Pelican Bay Clinic, Linda speaking.'

Jacob gave Fran a tour of the clinic, checking to see how she was taking it as they went. She seemed calm on the surface, but every now and again her eyes would flicker and her body would stiffen until she snapped herself out of it.

'That's the kitchen out there and the bathroom to the right,' he said. 'The portable X-ray machine is in the other consulting room. This room is yours.' He pushed open the door and waited for her to go in.

Fran took a step inside, smelling the clinic smells, feeling a little of her anguish easing. 'It's certainly well contained,' she said.

'It's not what you're used to, by any means, but maybe right now that's a good thing.'

She turned and smiled at him. 'Thanks for being here, for helping me settle in. I think I'll be fine. I had a quick glance in the waiting room. I think most of the patients are probably here to get prescriptions filled, having been so long without a doctor in town.'

'I'll be out back if you need me,' he said. 'I have some calls to make to do with the hit and run.'

'I don't expect you to stay all day.' She gave him a brave smile. 'I'll be fine. The worst is over now, I think.'

He brushed a strand of her hair back from her face. 'Don't forget about our date tonight. Do you want me to pick you up?'

'No, I'm not sure how long I will be here. Maybe it's better if I come under my own steam.'

He leaned forward and pressed a soft kiss to the middle of her forehead. 'I'm just a phone call away, don't forget that, OK?'

She smiled. 'OK.'

Fran made her way back to the waiting room and called out the first patient's name. 'Mrs Newman?'

Kate Newman was a woman in her mid-fifties with chronic back pain. From what Fran quickly read in the notes, several procedures had been done with little improvement. Three bilateral facet blocks at L4 and L5 had been performed in Sydney but Kate was still in need of narcotic pain relief.

'I'm nearly going crazy with this,' she said, wincing as she shifted in the chair. 'I can't do half the things I used to do. I can't even carry the washing out to the clothesline.'

'Back pain is quite debilitating,' Fran said. 'I see here from the notes you have arthritis. You saw a specialist in January. Has anyone suggested you see the neurosurgeon again for a new assessment?'

'There's been no one here to suggest anything,' Kate said. 'The last doctor gave me a few repeats of the painkiller but I'm down to my last two tablets.'

Fran reached for the prescription pad and once she had filled it out she quickly typed a referral letter on the computer on the desk. 'I think it's time you saw the specialist again for further advice on how to manage this disc,' she said. 'There are various things he might suggest, a discogram for one.

That's where they inject dye into the disc under X-ray to see how badly damaged it is. MRIs show us a lot of structural detail, but as you are lying down when the images are taken, they don't always show the full story.'

'Will I need surgery?' Kate asked, her expression showing her trepidation. 'The previous locum mentioned something about a fusion.'

'It could be you will have to have a fusion done, or perhaps a disc replacement,' Fran said. 'The surgery is very successful in cases like yours. It's just bad luck that disc is causing you so much trouble.'

'I slipped going down a ramp at our beach-house a few years ago and came down heavily on my backside,' Kate said. 'I've had trouble ever since.'

Fran handed her the letter of referral along with the prescription. 'I hope you can get in to see the neurosurgeon quickly,' she said. 'He's a very skilled man, one of the very best in his field. He operates at Sydney Metropolitan as well as a couple of private hospitals.'

'Thank you so much,' Kate said, wincing again as she rose from the chair. 'It's just so wonderful of you to fill in for us like this. How are your sister and the babes?'

'They're doing well,' Fran answered. 'I talked to her on the phone earlier. She would love to be home with them both, of course, but that's not possible just yet.'

'I had a premmie,' Kate said, placing her handbag strap over her shoulder. 'My firstborn son. Rob is now thirty years old and six foot tall and ninety kilos. He was the length of that pen of yours when he was born and weighed less than five hundred grams. No one thought he would make it.'

Fran smiled as she moved across to open the consulting-room door for Kate. It was so good to hear of the successes.

She had seen all too many of the not so successful. 'It's amazing how well the little ones get on, especially with all the technological advances in neonatal care,' she said. 'I hope things go well with the neurosurgical consult, Mrs Newman. Come back any time if you need more pain relief.'

Kate's brown eyes lit up. 'You mean you're thinking of staying permanently?'

Fran's smile faded. 'Um…no. I…um…haven't made any firm commitment as yet…'

'Well, I think you'd be perfect for the position,' Kate said warmly. 'I've heard nothing but nice things about you. Not only that, you've already got family here. Believe you me, that counts for a heck of a lot. My Rob and James and Tim all live interstate. I miss them so much and with my back the way it is, I haven't been able to travel so often to see them. Think about it, Dr Nin, please?'

'I will,' Fran said. 'It's just a big decision and I don't want to rush into anything.'

'Of course, it would make it easier for you if there was a young man here to tempt you into staying,' Kate said with a twinkling look. 'I saw that handsome Sergeant Hawke come into the clinic with you earlier. Are you and he an item?'

Fran could feel her colour rising. 'Oh, no, nothing like that,' she said, perhaps too quickly, a little too fervently.

'He's only been here a few months but he's already done so much for the community,' Kate said. 'He organised a working bee for the Pelican Bay children's park. He got rid of the old and dangerous rusty swings and slide, and with a couple of the other men, including my husband Bill, built a whiz-bang climbing frame and cubby house. You've got to love a man who's good with his hands, don't you think?'

'Um…yes…'

* * *

Kate was still smiling as she left and Fran was still blushing as she picked up the next patient's file. Jacob was on his mobile and gave Fran a quick glance as he came through Reception. He covered the phone and spoke to her out of earshot of Linda and the waiting room. 'Sorry, Fran, I've got to get back to the station to see to something urgent. I can send Constable Jeffrey over if you'd like.'

Fran shook her head. 'No, that's not necessary. I'm doing really well. I spoke with Linda a few minutes ago. Most of the patients just want prescriptions renewed.'

'I'll see you later, then,' he said, and, lifting his hand in a wave at Linda, left the clinic.

Fran let out a fluttering little breath and turned to face the waiting room. 'Tara Clark?' she called, scanning the area for the thin girl she had met at the general store a few days ago.

Tara was at the back of the waiting room, again dressed in loose-fitting black clothes in spite of the heat. On hearing her name called, she passed through the waiting-room crowd like a wraith, her head down, her bony shoulders like the wings of a bird.

'Hi, Tara,' Fran said as she led the way to the consulting room, closing the door firmly once they were inside. 'I met you the other day at the general store.'

Tara's dark gaze flicked away from Fran's as she sat on the edge of the seat near the desk. 'Yeah, I remember.'

'What can I do for you?' Fran asked, after quickly glancing at the notes. The file was thin, like Tara. One-sheet-of-paper thin. The last time she had been to the clinic had been more than three years ago when she'd been thirteen.

'I need something to help me sleep,' the young girl mumbled, without meeting Fran's gaze.

Fran felt alarm bells start to clang inside her head. 'You're quite young to be experiencing insomnia. How long have you had trouble with sleeping, Tara?'

A thin shoulder came up and went down in a shrug. 'A while.'

Fran mentally drummed her fingers on the desk. She knew from what Beryl had said in one of her recent gossip sessions that Tara lived on an outlying property with her father and brother. Her mother had left Tara's father for another man. The community had been shocked that a mother would abandon her children. Nola Clark hadn't wanted custody, she hadn't even wanted access visits. She had made a new life with her lover in another state, and apart from the occasional birthday card, which usually arrived late, she made no effort to contact her son and daughter.

Fran couldn't think of how different her upbringing had been. Her parents were still devoted to each other and her and Caro, their love totally unconditional and unending. They were even at this minute coming home early from their much-anticipated and meticulously planned trip abroad to be with Caro and the babies, putting their lives on hold just as they had for Fran when she had been attacked.

'Tara,' Fran began carefully, 'sleep medication is meant to be a very temporary thing to reset your body sleep rhythms. But if you are not sleeping and haven't been for a while, it might be better in the long term if you talked to someone about what might be causing the insomnia.'

Tara's smoky eyes hit hers. 'I'm not going to a counsellor,' she said with an adamant set to her mouth. 'Anyway, there isn't one here.'

'No, I know, but there are good people in Wollongong and—'

'I'm not going to talk to anyone.' This time the girl's tone was even more strident.

Fran quickly back-pedalled. 'OK, I understand. It's not easy talking to complete strangers about very personal stuff.'

'It's not about *her*,' Tara said with a curl of her lip over the word.

Fran waited a beat. 'Your mother, you mean?'

The smoky eyes burned with bitterness. 'I *hate* her. She left my dad. She wrecked his life. She wrecked all of our lives.'

Fran felt the girl's pain coming off her in waves of negative energy. She could see the little child inside the teenage body. The little lost girl who probably still cried for her mother at night. The little girl who had felt she had to step up into her mother's role and take care of her brother and devastated father. The little girl who was trying to find her place in the world as a young woman, but not quite making it.

'Tara,' she said gently. 'I noticed the other day you have some scars on your wrists.'

Tara's expression darkened defensively. 'So?'

'Do you want to tell me about how you got them?'

Tara held Fran's gaze for a full thirty seconds before she finally dropped hers, her voice coming out in a fractured whisper. 'I can't help it… I just have to do it… It gets rid of the pain…'

Fran swallowed the ridge of emotion that had risen in her throat. It was so important to keep in control clinically but this young girl was such a tragic case. Her isolation added to her pain, making Fran suddenly realise how significant it was that Tara had made the appointment to see her. She had to handle this carefully; she had this one chance to build up trust and rapport so the young girl could share some of the burdens she carried. 'Self-mutilation is very common, Tara,' she said, 'especially in your age group.'

Tara's eyes met hers. 'Is it?'

Fran nodded. 'Of course it's not an ideal way to handle

stress but it's a well-recognised one.' She waited a beat before continuing. 'It's a bit like nail-biting. It becomes a habit that's hard to break. It's important to get control of it, though. Talking about the issues that are worrying you is probably the best approach. I know you don't want to involve a counsellor but maybe we can come to some arrangement.'

Fran didn't stop to think of the propriety of what she was about to propose, she felt too compelled to do something, *anything*, to help this young girl. 'I'm not planning on working here at the clinic, I'm just filling in for the one day, but I will be in town for the next couple of months. We can just meet up informally, you know, go for walks on the beach, chat about stuff, anything you like, in total confidence.'

Tara shifted in her seat, her eyes going to the scars on her wrists, as if checking to see if they were still there. After a moment she looked up with those pain-filled eyes of hers to meet Fran's. 'I hate myself,' she said. 'I've always felt if I was different, she wouldn't have left.'

'A lot of kids blame themselves when their parents break up,' Fran said softly. 'But adults have issues kids often know very little about, issues that usually go way back to before the kids were born.'

Tara flicked her tongue across her paper-dry, pale, anaemic-looking lips. 'I'm worried about my dad. He punched Sergeant Hawke in the face the other day.' She looked at Fran with fear shadowing her eyes. 'I'm worried he might send my dad to jail.'

Fran felt something shift inside her chest. 'I can speak to Sergeant Hawke if you like,' she said. 'Would you like me to do that?'

'Would you?' Tara asked, hope like a tiny candle flame flickering in her eyes.

Fran smiled. 'Of course I don't mind. Sergeant Hawke strikes me as the sort of man who would be very understanding about what's been going on at home. Leave it with me, Tara.'

She reached for a tourniquet and a syringe. 'Now, let's run a couple of blood tests on you to see what your haemoglobin level is and your iron levels and stuff. You might be anaemic, which will make you feel tired during the day, which in turn could influence how well you sleep at night. The new doctor who eventually takes up the position can follow you up if you need supplements.'

Tara reluctantly rolled up her sleeve and Fran's stomach gave a savage clench as she saw the criss-cross of scars that went almost up to the elbow. She carefully drew up the blood, chatting to Tara as she capped each sample tube. The girl seemed to relax a little as the consultation went on, and after Fran had organised a walk on the beach in a few days' time, Tara even stretched her pale lips into a tentative smile.

Fran chewed the end of her pen once Tara had left. She hoped she was doing the right thing in organising informal contact with the young teenager. At least she could talk to Jacob about it, she thought. Perhaps he would know how best to deal with the situation.

She put the pen down and ran her tongue across her lips, remembering how wonderful it had felt to have his mouth on hers. She sat dreamily for several moments until the intercom buzzed her out of her reverie.

'Sorry, Linda,' she said, tucking her hair behind her ear in a distracted manner. 'I'm coming right now.'

The last patient of the day was a young teenage mother who came in with a toddler who was running a fever. The little boy was listless and clingy but brightened up a bit when Fran handed him a toy to hold while she examined his ears and listened to his chest.

'How long has he been feeling unwell?' Fran asked the mother.

'Most of this week, but as I don't drive I couldn't take him anywhere else to see a doctor,' the young woman, called Beth Judd, explained.

As Fran handed the child back to his mother she noticed he winced when she touched his left arm. On closer inspection she noticed it was slightly swollen. 'How long has Kane's arm been sore?'

The young mother flushed and adjusted the child's T-shirt. 'I can't remember... He fell over, I think.'

Fran quickly glanced at the notes but there was nothing written there to suggest anything had happened to the child that could have been caused by maltreatment. The little boy looked well cared for, and Beth, though not much older than eighteen or so, looked well groomed, though a little tired from caring for a sick toddler.

'I think we should do a quick X-ray just to make sure it's not broken,' Fran said. 'He's not using it the same as his other arm—see how he's holding that toy?'

The mother looked distinctly uncomfortable all the time the X-ray was being processed. When Fran showed the evidence of a non-deformed greenstick fracture of the wrist, Beth's face turned almost sheet-white.

'Does Kane's father live with you?' Fran asked.

Beth brushed her son's blond wispy hair back from his forehead. 'No, he left when I got pregnant,' she said. 'I've got a new partner now.'

'How does he get on with Kane?' Fran asked, reaching to

tickle the little boy under the chin before she began to apply a cast to his arm.

Beth still wouldn't meet Fran's eyes the whole time she worked on Kane's arm. Instead, she concentrated on picking bits of lint off his clothes. 'All right, I guess,' she said. 'Kane's not his kid so it's hard for him to love him like I do.'

'There is nothing quite like a mother's love, is there?' Fran asked, this time managing to capture Beth's gaze momentarily. 'Does your mother live nearby?'

Beth shifted her gaze again. 'No...' She began to toy with the tiny laces on her little son's shoes. 'She hasn't spoken to me since I told her I was pregnant. She wanted me to get rid of him so I could finish school and go to university.' She looked at Fran. 'I left it a bit late in any case. I didn't know I was pregnant until I was almost four months gone. My mother tried to make me give him up for adoption but I didn't want him to grow up without knowing who I was, you know?'

Fran touched the young woman on the arm. 'I understand,' she said gently. 'It's a big decision, no matter what you choose to do.'

Beth stroked her little son's head again. 'I just want him to have a good life...to be happy.'

'It's what we all want, Beth,' Fran said. It was hard not to let her thoughts run through various scenarios over how Kane had injured himself. Beth's nervousness could be read so many ways. A young single mother had a lot to deal with without the shadow of suspicion of physical abuse cast over her. Fran knew she had to tread carefully in case the young mother lost trust in her. Calling in the authorities too early was sometimes almost as bad as calling them in too late. She had to establish trust and see if there was any valid reason to suspect maltreatment. Toddlers often had falls, sometimes quite nasty ones. It was a part of growing up and discovering their world.

'Kane has a nasty throat,' she said as she reached for the prescription pad. 'I'm prescribing something and someone will need to see him here in a couple of days. Tonsillitis can sometimes go to the chest so I would like the doctor who takes over to keep a close watch on him.' She picked up the phone and organised a time with Linda for a follow-up appointment to ensure Kane was seen again.

'Thanks, Linda.' Fran put the phone down and handed Beth a card with the date and time of the next appointment written on it. 'I bet this young man will be feeling a whole lot better by then, but come back and see the new doctor in any case as it's time for a weight and height check and it's important to see if his arm has improved.'

Beth cuddled her son close, a changing-bag slung over one of her shoulders, her handbag over the other. 'Thanks for seeing him,' she said. 'It's been hard, waiting so long for a new doctor to arrive.'

Fran smiled thinly. 'Well, I'm only doing the one shift. There is a new doctor on his way. He's due a week on Monday, I believe.'

Beth shifted her weight. 'I heard your sister had twins,' she said.

'Yes, little boys,' Fran said. 'They won't be coming home for a while yet though. They're two months premature but doing very well.'

Beth tugged at her bottom lip with her teeth. 'It's good she's got you to help her…you know, when she comes home with them. One baby's tough, I don't think I could handle two at once.'

Fran sat back down, hoping Beth would do the same, but

she remained standing, with Kane tucked on her hip. 'Did you have anyone to help you when Kane was born?' she asked.

Beth shook her head, a shadow of sadness sweeping over her face like a cloud moving past the sun. 'No one living with me. I had a nice neighbour who used to help me occasionally, but she died last year. She was in her eighties. I don't know the neighbours where we live now. We live out near the old quarry at Bellbird Gully. It's kind of isolated, not the sort of place to chat over the fence with the neighbours.'

'You and Kane must miss your friend,' Fran said. 'My sister and I had a similar surrogate granny when we were growing up in Melbourne. She adored children, even though she had never married or had any of her own.'

Kane began to grizzle and Beth moved towards the door. 'Thanks again, Dr Nin,' she said. 'Maybe I'll see you around town some time before you leave.'

'I am sure you will,' Fran said, smiling as she held the door open. She closed it once the young mother had left and, leaning her back against the wood to give her leg a rest, felt a small frown pull at her brows…

CHAPTER NINE

FRAN was only ten minutes late getting to Jacob's house. She had rushed back home to let Rufus out for a run and had quickly changed into gym gear.

She pulled in behind Jacob's police vehicle in the driveway and made her way to the front door. He opened it before she knocked; he had obviously only just returned home himself for he was still dressed in his uniform, his gunbelt strapped to his lean waist.

'Hi. Glad you made it,' he said, his gaze running over her form. 'How did the rest of the clinic go?'

'Fine,' she said, feeling her lips tingle when she looked at his mouth. He was in need of a shave—the dark shadow looked so sexy on him she could barely stop herself from reaching up to touch his face. She wondered if he was going to kiss her in greeting. She stood uncertainly, not sure if she should make the first move. It had been so long since she had dated. She didn't know the protocol any more. It made her feel about sixteen, gauche and shy and awkward.

The cool air-conditioned ambience wrapped around Fran's hot face and body, but even so the atmosphere seemed charged with pulsing warmth. She felt it when her eyes connected with Jacob's brilliant blue ones. It was like looking at the centre of a gas-powered flame.

'Would you like a cool drink before we get started in the gym?' he asked.

'I had some water in the car before I came…thanks,' she said, following him to a large atrium where he had set up his state-of-the-art gym equipment.

'Ever used a leg press before?' Jacob asked.

'I've never really been a gym bunny,' she confessed with a little grimace. 'I used to jog a bit before…' She paused, her expression clouding before she continued, 'Before I was injured.'

Jacob led her to the leg press and set the weights to a light load. He showed her how to work her muscles, slowly and in a controlled way, to get the most benefit. 'That's it,' he said as she got into a rhythm. 'Nice and easy to begin with.'

She gave him a self-conscious glance, but after a few more exercises on the other equipment she seemed to get into the swing of things. Her cheeks were slightly flushed as he brought the routine to an end, her top lip shiny with tiny droplets of perspiration. He wanted to press his mouth to hers, to taste her again, but he hadn't yet showered or shaved. He could still see the faint mark he had made on her skin the evening before. It made his insides clench to think of how tiny and fragile she was compared to him.

'Best not to overdo it the first time,' he said, handing her a bottle of water.

Her eyes fell away from his as her fingers brushed against his when she took the bottle of water from him. 'Yes…'

He scraped a hand through his sticky hair. 'Would you mind if I had a quick shower?' he asked. 'You can head out to the deck if you like. I won't be long.'

* * *

Fran took the chilled bottle of water out to the deck, breathing in the sea breeze as she opened the sliding doors. The cockatoos were nowhere to be seen this time, but a kookaburra was perched in a eucalypt about fifty metres away, its distinctive chortle echoing across the gully.

Within a few minutes the doors leading to the deck opened and Jacob appeared. His hair was still damp, the deep grooves of a comb clearly visible amongst the thick black strands. His jaw was cleanly shaven and the scent of his lemon-based aftershave curled around her nostrils, making her think of citrus groves in summer. He was dressed in blue denim jeans and a black T-shirt, showcasing his muscular form and the healthy colour of his skin. It was almost painful to look and not to touch, Fran thought.

'Sorry about that,' he said, taking the seat next to her. 'I don't feel really human until I've washed off the blood and sweat of the day.'

Fran couldn't have asked for a better cue, considering the conversation she'd had with Tara Clark earlier that afternoon. 'I had Tara Clark come to see me today,' she said. 'I believe you know her father.'

One of his fingers absently felt for the healing cut on his cheekbone. 'Yeah, you could say that.'

She took a breath and continued. 'Are you thinking of pressing charges?'

He shifted his lips in a couldn't-be-bothered-with-the-paperwork manner. 'No. He's not a bad bloke, just down on his luck. I just caught him on a bad day.'

'That's very magnanimous of you, considering he could have seriously injured your eye,' she said.

He looked out to the sea, his forehead creasing slightly. 'It's his son Sam I'm more concerned about.' He looked back at Fran. 'Tara, too, when it comes to that. She seems a bit of a lost soul right now.'

Fran knew she was walking a fine line on the issue of patient confidentiality but she rationalised that Jacob was already concerned about the family and he was a senior police officer to boot. 'I don't know much about the brother but, like you, I am very concerned about Tara,' she said. 'So concerned I've decided to spend some time with her, not as a doctor or anything, more as a friend.'

He absorbed her statement with a slight elevation of his dark brows. 'She must have really got to you,' he said.

Fran blew out her cheeks on a sigh. 'She did.'

'You happen to see the scars on her arms?' he asked.

She nodded. 'She's been self-mutilating a long time, by the looks of things. She needs regular counselling. I'm not exactly qualified but she refuses to see anyone else. I was lucky she agreed to see me on an informal basis. She hasn't been to the clinic in years.'

'I'm sure you'll do a good job supporting her while you're here,' he said. 'She needs a reliable female role model. Wayne tries his best but from what I've observed he hasn't got over his wife's desertion so he's not been much help to his kids.'

Fran sighed again. 'It's sad, isn't it? What happens to people, I mean. One minute their life is going fine and the next it's ruined.'

'Yeah.'

She looked up at him. 'Jacob, how well do you know Beth Judd?'

He frowned as if trying to place the name. 'I've only been in the Bay five months so I haven't met everyone unless they come to my attention.'

Fran lifted her brows at that. 'You mean, unless they break the law?'

He did that thing with his lips that was almost but not quite a smile. 'I admit I am not the most sociable person in town, Fran. I like my own space too much. But tell me, what are your concerns about the woman you mentioned?'

Fran let out a sigh. 'I could be imagining things, of course, but she is a young mother, about eighteen, with a toddler of almost two, a little boy called Kane. He came in with a green-stick fracture of his wrist. It wasn't the reason she brought him in to see me either.'

Jacob's expression became cop-like. 'Do you think she hurt the child?'

Fran shrugged. 'I don't think so, but who can be sure? Kids often hurt themselves, especially toddlers.'

'That was her story, was it?'

She nodded, chewing at her lip.

'Does she have a partner?' he asked.

'Yes, but not the boy's father,' she answered. 'She sort of hinted at how hard it was for him to love the child as it wasn't his.'

'Kids deserve to be loved, no matter who they belong to.'

Fran looked up at him but he was looking into the distance, his eyes narrowed against the glare of the sun. Her heart gave a tiny flutter when his eyes came back to hers, her stomach lifting and falling like an elevator that had slipped between floors.

'What's the partner's name?' Jacob asked.

'I don't know,' she answered. 'It wasn't in the notes and I didn't think to ask.'

Something in his eyes made Fran feel defensive. 'I didn't want to lose her trust,' she said. 'I started to feel a rapport with her and I didn't want to jeopardise it. I don't think it's right to suspect everyone who walks in the door. First impressions can be very misleading.'

'Is she coming to see you again?'

Fran felt her back come up. 'No. I'm not taking on the position, Jacob. I just did one session, that doesn't mean I'm under contract for the next ten years.'

The air seemed to crackle with tension.

'Did you make an appointment for her to see someone else?' Jacob broke the stiff silence.

'Yes,' Fran said, still bristling. 'The new doctor is due to arrive in a little over a week's time.'

'Do you think she will keep the appointment with someone she doesn't know?'

She bit her lip again, releasing it to say, 'I hope so.'

'So in the meantime, a little kid barely old enough to speak is living with some guy who might be abusing him?' he said, looking down at her with those dark-rimmed eyes piercing hers.

Fran felt her back come up again. 'Look, I did what I thought was appropriate for now,' she said. 'The child looks well cared for apart from an infection, which any child can suffer from. I just thought I'd mention it to you in case you had any background information on the mother or her situation.'

'I don't, but I will,' he said with a determined set to his jaw.

Another silence tightened the air, so much so even the birds went silent.

'You think I'm a coward for not taking on the position, don't you?' Fran said, unable to prevent a scowl distorting her mouth.

He gave her a frustrated look. 'Did I say that?'

'You didn't have to—I can see it in your face. You think one little hand-holding session is going to fix me? It doesn't work that way, Jacob. I might never get over this.'

'I think you're getting a little too attached to the victim role,' he said. 'For a start, you're talking yourself into failure.'

She got to her feet and slammed the cup on the table beside the lounger. 'I think it's time I left.'

Jacob blocked her exit. 'Wait a damn minute, Fran. What the hell has got into you?'

Fran felt her emotions slipping out of control. 'I can't do this, Jacob. I don't know if I can cope with your expectations as well as my own.'

He brought her hand up to his mouth, pressing his warm lips to her bent fingers as his eyes continued to hold hers. 'Hey, listen to me, sweetheart. I am not expecting anything from you. I think you were amazing today. You walked into that clinic and saw every single patient. You made a lot of people happy, maybe even saved a life or two.'

Her bottom lip was still pushed out in a pout. 'But I can't help thinking you, like just about everyone else in Pelican Bay, think I should be the one who takes up the position.'

'Yeah, well, I can't speak for everyone else but my reasons for wanting you to stay have absolutely nothing to do with my need of a doctor.'

She gave a little lift of her shoulders. 'Everyone needs a check-up, even disgustingly healthy people like you.'

'So check me over,' he said, bringing her hands to his chest. 'I have this little pain here.'

She frowned. 'Where?'

He placed her hand over his beating heart. 'There, right there. It feels like someone's got it in a vice.'

Fran felt her own heart contract at the huskiness in his tone. 'I don't actually have a stethoscope on me right now,' she said, staring at his mouth.

'Then we'll have to leave that part of the examination for

another time,' he said, running his hands down to hold her hands in his. 'You do realise in a place like Pelican Bay it will be hard to keep our dating a secret, don't you?'

Fran widened her eyes at him. '*Are* we dating?'

He smiled that unreadable half-smile again. 'You're here, I'm here, and we're alone. That sounds like a date to me.'

She ran her tongue over her lips. 'Oh…well, then…'

He brought her a little closer, his hands going to the curve at the base of her spine. Sensations spiralled through her at the intimate contact with his hard male body, making her heart start to race out of control.

'Of course, we could just be friends if you'd prefer it,' he said as he brushed his lips against the sensitive skin of her neck.

'Um…I—I already have plenty of friends,' Fran said, her whole body shivering with delight as his lips moved to just below her ear lobe.

'Me, too,' he said, moving upwards to kiss the corner of her mouth.

Fran was nearly going crazy to feel his lips on hers. He was so close, tantalisingly so. Every nerve began to quiver with the need to feel the pressure of him, the heat and fire of his taste and touch.

Suddenly he was there.

His mouth captured hers in a searing kiss that sent arrows of heat to her core. His tongue didn't ask for entry, it demanded it, sweeping hers into a bone-shuddering dance of desire that left her breathless. She clung to him, unable to support herself under the sensual onslaught. Her senses sang with delight as he pressed her closer against him, the hot, hard heat of him a heady reminder of the fierce attraction that had simmered between them from the first moment they had met.

When his hands moved from the small of her back to cup her breasts she gave a soft whimper of pleasure. His caressing touch was gentle but possessive, a thrilling combination that made her body hum with sensation. Her nipples budded under the rolling action of his thumbs, her belly becoming a melting pool of longing.

He lifted his mouth from hers for a moment, his breathing not quite steady. 'I don't know what it is about you but every time I see you I can't seem to keep my hands off you.'

A little smile played about her mouth as she linked her arms around his neck, her body sliding against the length of him, making his eyes flare with desire. 'Same goes,' she said in a husky tone.

'That's good to hear,' he said, lifting her off her feet.

'Oh!' Fran gasped.

He frowned. 'Did I hurt you?' ·

'No, of course not. It's just I'm not used to being swept off my feet.'

His eyes glinted down at her. 'Is that what's happening?'

She chewed at her lip, her gaze dipping to his mouth, a frown tugging at her brow. 'I'm not sure…maybe…'

He set her back down, his hold only slackening when he was sure she was steady on her feet. 'This is a little too soon for you, isn't it?' he asked.

Fran gave him a rueful look, her face feeling hot. 'You must think I'm a prude.'

'Not at all,' he said, sliding his warm hands down her arms to loosely encircle her wrists. 'You've been through a hell of lot lately. It's totally understandable you would be cautious as a result.'

'Caro thinks I should have a red-hot affair to boost my confidence,' she said.

'Sounds like good advice to me.'

Her look was wry. 'Yes, well, it would to a man. But I'm not really wired that way. I suspect a lot of women aren't.'

He released her wrists and stepped back from her. 'Not all men are after one-night stands,' he said. 'I would eventually like to have what my parents had. They were friends as well as lovers. After my father was killed my mother never looked at another man. He was the love of her life. I admired that commitment. She was still young and attractive, she could have had another chance at happiness, but she loved my father too much to even consider it.'

'My parents have a similar relationship,' Fran said. 'I can't imagine what either one would do if something happened to the other. It must have been so hard for you and your mother when your father died.'

He held her look for a lengthy moment without speaking, a shadow of something moving in his eyes.

'I was meant to be working with him that evening,' he finally said, his tone weighted with regret.

Fran frowned at him. 'You're surely not blaming yourself?'

His expression was still grim. 'What would it have cost me to give up watching a movie with some mates?'

'It could have cost you your life,' she pointed out.

He dismissed that with a wave of his hand. 'I should have been there. I might have been able to save him if I had been.'

'I can understand how you would feel that way, but you might not have been able to do anything for him,' she said.

'Something would have been better than nothing,' he said, raking a hand through his hair. 'I wasn't much better at looking out for my mother when it came to the end. She died before I could get there.'

She moved towards him and touched him on the forearm.

'Not everyone can make it in time. The important thing is she knew you were thinking of her. Think of all you did for her here. It was just bad luck things didn't work out the way you both wanted it to.' She took a little breath and added, 'If I had been here while she was here, I would have seen her and treated her. I would have fought back my fears for you and for her.'

He placed his hand over hers, squeezing it softly. 'Thanks, that means a lot to me. I think she would have liked you. She would have certainly been impressed with your baking abilities. She made the best cakes, or so I thought until I tasted yours.'

Fran smiled up at him. 'Wait until you taste my double chocolate macadamia nut cookies.'

He smiled in return. 'Speaking of food, I guess I should get started on our dinner.'

'What can I do to help?' Fran asked, trying not to stare at his mouth. She wanted to stand on tiptoe and press her lips to his, to finish what they had started minutes earlier. *Was* it too soon? How did one measure such a thing? She was as fiercely attracted to Jacob as he was to her. She could see it in his eyes every time they met hers. It felt as if she had come into contact with a live power line. Her body fizzed all over with sensation, the blood in her veins rocketing through at breakneck speed.

'For a start, you could help by not looking at me like that,' he said with a wry slant of a smile.

She felt her cheeks begin to flush all over again. 'I'm sorry…was it that obvious?'

He tipped up her chin to lock gazes with her, his finger like a fiery brand on her skin. 'It might be too soon for both of us but I want you.'

The bald statement made Fran's eyes flare. Her belly gave a little kick of excitement and a pulse-like ache began deep and low inside her. 'I want you too.' Her voice came out husky and soft and breathless.

'The way I see it, we have two choices,' he said, still holding her gaze. 'One: we step back right now before we go any further.'

'And…and two?' Again Fran's voice was so husky it was barely audible.

His pupils were like black holes in a startlingly blue ocean. 'Two: we kiss again and see what happens.'

She moistened her lips with the tip of her tongue, trying to sound casual and easygoing about it all. 'Sounds like a plan.'

His gaze went to her mouth. 'I don't know about you but I'm leaning towards the kiss and see what happens.'

'Yeah, me too,' she whispered as his mouth hovered above hers.

When his lips came down over hers she felt giant shock waves of reaction course through her. His kiss was leisurely at first but then it changed to full-throttle passion, leaving her senses spinning. His tongue curled around hers, tasting her, exploring her until she was clinging to him unashamedly. Her body was on fire, she could feel the flames of desire licking at every secret place, her hunger for him ravenous. With his mouth still fused to hers, his hands slipped under her top, sliding up her bare flesh until he was cupping her breasts. Her nipples were painfully tight and she shuddered when his mouth left hers to suckle on each of them in turn over her top. She arched her spine, her breathing coming in short, sharp gasps as his tongue laved her, his freshly shaven skin still abrading her slightly. It was a delicious reminder of his maleness and her femininity, his hardness and her softness. It made her heart hammer with the thrill of expectation of how it would feel to be in his arms, skin on skin.

This time when he lifted her in his arms she simply laced her arms around his neck, relishing the strength of him as he carried her to the master bedroom.

He placed her on the mattress, coming down over her, his weight pinning her to the bed. His mouth came back to hers, sending her into another vortex of feeling as his hands slipped back under her top to possess her again.

She writhed beneath him restlessly, aching to do the same to him, to feel his nakedness, to explore the muscled contours of his body. Her hands searched for him, tugging his T-shirt out of his jeans, her palms sliding over the satin-covered steel of his chest and abdomen. The light dusting of masculine hair snagged on her fingertips, and she drew circles around his flat hard nipples, quivering with delight when he made a sound of pleasure at the back of his throat. Gaining confidence, she moved her hands downwards, undoing the fastening on his jeans, slowly rolling down the metal zipper, sensing the way his abdominal muscles clenched in anticipation as she came to the final barrier of his underwear. Her fingers brushed over him experimentally, her heart leaping at the length and latent power of him. She heard him suck in a breath as she rolled back the fabric of his underwear, her fingers dancing over him lightly.

He made another deep guttural sound as she enclosed him inside the warmth of her hand, tightening her hold, sliding up and down until he placed one of his hands over hers in order to keep control.

'Whoa, there,' he said, breathing heavily. 'I'm fully loaded and you're not even undressed. Let's even up things a bit.'

Fran felt her insides twist with longing as he started to work on her clothes. Her top went first, her bra next, freeing her breasts for his touch.

'Beautiful,' he murmured against her creamy flesh. 'So soft, just like silk.'

She felt her skin pop all over in goose-bumps when his mouth closed over each nipple in turn, the moist lave of his tongue making her spine arch like a cat. Sensations fired through her like fireworks exploding beneath her skin, leaving spot fires all over her flesh wherever his mouth kissed her.

He worked his way down from her breasts, helping her out of her gym pants, the soft little thuds of her trainers barely registering in her hearing as his mouth found the tiny bowl of her belly button. He dipped his tongue in before circling it, and then moving lower, millimetre by millimetre until he came to the scrap of lace she was wearing. She pulled in a ragged breath, her whole body bracing for his next move. She shuddered when he slowly peeled the lace away from her body, her senses so finely tuned to his touch her skin felt super-sensitive.

He cupped her with the palm of his hand, the warmth of him seeping through her tender flesh. Her whole being pulsed with longing and, as if sensing her need, he gently traced the feminine seam of her body before parting her to slowly glide one finger into her silky moistness. The sensation of being explored by him so intimately made her breath catch in her throat. He was so unhurried, so patient and yet so passionate in his every caress. Her body was alive with need, prickling with it, pulsing with it and aching for it to be brought to completion. She made a tiny sound of impatience and he smiled lazily as he moved back over her to cover his mouth with hers.

She gave herself up to the kiss, the weight of his naked

body over hers making her tingle all over. His chest hair tickled her breasts, and the steely flatness of his abdomen against her belly burned her skin until she could feel the moist beads of perspiration gathering between their bodies.

It was so primal, the way he was pinning her, his strong legs entwined with hers, the rough hair of his limbs contrasting with her smoothness, the friction of their bodies, straining to get closer, to get as close as physically possible. She felt giddy with anticipation, feverish and breathless and more than a little out of control. It was as if her body was ruling her mind. She was no longer the sensible, cautious woman of the past, a little shy and uncertain of herself. In Jacob's arms she was a wanton woman, not ashamed of showing how much she needed him. Her body was speaking for her, writhing beneath his for the final act of possession, her mouth feeding off his, her tongue licking and stroking his, her teeth biting at him in playful, kittenish bites that made him groan in response.

He lifted his mouth from hers and reached past her to open the bedside-table drawer, rummaging through the contents before he located a condom.

Fran tried not to think of who had been in his bed last. She didn't want to think of where she was located in the line of his past and future lovers. She daren't think too far ahead. For now all she wanted to concentrate on was how it felt to be the one he had right now.

He wanted her, he had told her and he had shown her in the most telling way possible. His body was straining to keep control; she felt the tension in him as she watched him apply the condom, the overwhelming need for release so like her own.

He moved back over her to kiss her again, his tongue playing with hers as he positioned his pelvis against hers.

She shifted her legs, her body opening to him instinctively as he possessed her in one deep slick thrust that knocked the air right out of her chest. She gasped as her body gripped him, each tender ridge of her feminine form holding him tightly as he moved within her. Hot sparks sizzled down her spine as he increased his pace, the rhythm of their rocking bodies making her sensitised nerves go into a frenzied spasm. She could feel the tension building in her body, the invisible strings of desire tightening like a violin being tuned after years of toneless laxity. Her whole body was humming, vibrating with her need of him.

He changed his rhythm, slow and easy and then faster, and then backing off again as if he was holding himself back from the edge. It thrilled her to think how affected he was by her. She had not thought of herself as irresistible before and yet in his arms she felt as if he was fighting for control every step of the way.

She loved the feel of him inside her, the smooth glide of him within her, the way he filled her, stretching her to accommodate him, making her feel totally his. Her body strained against him, searching for that extra pressure, aching for the final completion. She arched her back, groaning, whimpering, begging him to send her to paradise.

He reached down between their bodies and played her with his fingers, stroking her until she shuddered her way through an orgasm so intense she felt as if everything inside her head was spinning. Brilliant lights like thousands of camera flashes went off, heat coursing through her like liquid flames, searing her as she quivered and shook beneath his powerful body.

Fran was still floating back down from the ceiling when he gave a rough grunt as he tensed all over, every muscle pulled as tight as a bow before he surged forward, spilling himself, his body quaking with the after shocks of release. She felt every one of them reverberate through her body, sending waves of vicarious pleasure washing over her that she had brought him to this.

She held him to her, listening to his hectic breathing, her body still exquisitely sensitive where it was in intimate contact with his. She was reluctant to break the spell of intimacy that had woven them together. It felt so good to be in his arms, to be lying in the afterglow of spent passion, to feel him inside her, to feel satisfied in a way she had never felt before.

She felt a little embarrassed at her lack of experience. Had he been able to tell? she wondered. How mortifying if he had. She was a doctor, for pity's sake. How could she have lived this long and not realised what pleasure her body was capable of giving and receiving?

Jacob rolled away and discreetly disposed of the condom, turning back to lie on his side beside her, his fingers tracing a circular pattern on each of her slim hips in turn. He came to the scar at the top of her right thigh, noting how she tensed, as if preparing herself for his revulsion. 'It's just a scar, sweetheart,' he said. 'It'll fade in time.'

She averted her gaze from his, plucking at the sheet beneath her with her fingers, her teeth sinking into the flesh of her lips.

He frowned and angled her head so she had to face him eye to eye. 'Is everything all right?' he asked.

She gave him a forced smile. 'Of course.'

His frown deepened. 'I didn't hurt you, did I?'

She looked a little shocked at his question. 'No of course not! You were…' she gave a little shuddering sigh '…amazing…'

He brushed some wayward strands of her long hair off her face. 'When it comes to that, you were pretty amazing yourself.'

She dropped her gaze and her fingers began pulling at the sheet again. 'Jacob…I wouldn't like you to think I do this regularly…I mean, jump into bed with someone I barely know…'

He studied her for a moment. 'You're regretting what happened just now?' he asked.

Her eyes briefly met his. 'Are you?'

'You should know better than to ask a man that after he's just had mind-blowing sex with a beautiful woman,' he remarked dryly.

She bit her lip again, her eyes falling away from his as she moved away from him to gather up her clothes. 'I just want to know…'

Jacob frowned and reached for one of her arms to hold her steady so she had to face him. 'Know what?' he asked.

Her eyes contained a spark of insecurity and fear. 'How much of what happened just now was attraction and how much was pity?'

His frowned deepened. 'You think I made love to you out of pity?'

'I don't know.' Fran felt her eyes sting with unshed tears. 'I just don't want to be used. I don't want to be hurt and I don't want anyone to feel sorry for me.'

His frown disappeared as he stepped back into her personal space. He took her hands in his and held them up against his chest. 'Do you want to know why I made love to you?' he asked.

She gave a little nod, blinking back the hot scald of tears.

'This is why,' he said, and brought his mouth down to hers.

CHAPTER TEN

FRAN sighed as his lips moved against hers with exquisite tenderness. It was so easy to imagine he was falling in love with her when he kissed her like that.

Falling in love?

The words rang like clanging bells inside her head. Was that what she wanted from him, to fall in love with her as she was falling in love with him? How had that happened? One minute she had hated him…well, maybe not exactly hated him, disliked was probably a more accurate term, but how could she possibly have fallen in love with him?

Easily, she thought as he deepened the kiss, sending her senses into another whirlwind of feeling. How could she not fall in love with him? He was the most magnetic man she had ever met. She had felt the powerful pull of attraction almost from the first moment she had met him, and each day since had only intensified the feelings she had tried to ignore. But whether he had similar feelings for her was only speculation at this stage. She knew enough about men to know they were primarily ruled by their bodies, not their hearts.

Jacob was a single man, a gorgeous single man currently living in a quiet seaside town where meeting young women of a suitable age was far more difficult than in the big city. He had mentioned he had broken things off with his ex-girlfriend a few months ago, which more or less explained his readiness to conduct a short-term affair with *her*. What full-blooded man wouldn't fancy a quick fling if one was in the offing?

Fran cringed at the thought of how easily she had succumbed to his advances. She knew it was more or less de rigueur these days for young women to sleep with a man after only a couple of dates, but she had never felt the urge to do so before now. Something about Jacob had made the sensible part of her brain short-circuit. With one look from those blue eyes of his she had become a melting pool of shameless longing.

Desire whipped through her each time his tongue brushed against hers. His lips were like fire against her mouth, branding her with his taste, making her feelings for him impossible to ignore. She clung to him, pressing herself against his rock-hard pelvis, her half-dressed state somehow making it all the more exciting. He was wearing his jeans but his chest was still bare and rubbed against her breasts, making her flesh tingle with sensitivity.

The sound of a phone ringing made Jacob reluctantly break the kiss. 'Sorry,' he said, reaching for his mobile where he had left it earlier. 'I'd better get this.'

The interruption was exactly what Fran needed to get herself back into her clothes and back into her rational mind. Things had moved so quickly in such a short space of time she was having trouble keeping up. She felt dazed, both physically and mentally. Jacob's love-making had overwhelmed her in every way possible. She was shocked by how she had responded to him. She was doubly shocked that she had been set to respond to him all over again if it hadn't been for the phone call he'd received.

Once Jacob ended the call he unzipped his jeans and quickly exchanged them for his police uniform, strapping on his gunbelt before reaching for his hat. 'Sorry about this, Fran,' he said. 'Can we have a rain-check on dinner?'

'That's fine,' she said. 'I should get back to Rufus in any case. He gets into mischief when there's no one around to keep an eye on him.'

Jacob bent down and brushed his mouth against hers. 'I'll call you tomorrow.'

Fran drove home with her lips still buzzing and her body still tingling. A slow smile spread over her face as she thought of the next few months in Pelican Bay spending time with Jacob, the first man she had ever loved.

Fran was just coming out of the general store late the following morning when she ran into Jim Broderick, Candi's father.

'Dr Nin?' He took off his hat, fumbling with the rim of it between his fingers. 'I was wondering if you had a minute for a chat. I tried to book at the clinic but Linda said you weren't seeing any more patients.'

Fran felt the now all-too-familiar twinge of guilt but somehow stood her ground. 'No, that's right,' she said. 'The new locum is on his or her way in the next week or so.'

'The thing is…I don't know what to do about Candi.' He rubbed his weatherworn face with one of his equally worn hands. 'Ever since she came home from hospital she's been impossible to live with. She won't eat, or at least not when I'm around. She won't go to school and she won't even look at me, much less speak to me.'

Fran grimaced in empathy. 'She's at a difficult age, and

breaking her leg and losing her horse would have hit her hard. Teenagers tend to see things as very black and white. Give her time. Once she's more mobile she will bounce back, I'm sure.'

He released a heavy sigh. 'I had no choice but to put the poor horse out of its misery. His back leg was broken. But she won't listen to me.'

'Mr Broderick…Jim.' Fran reached forward to touch him on the arm. 'You did the right thing. It would have been cruel to allow him to suffer. In time Candi will understand that. She is grieving, perhaps not just for Cheeky but maybe for her mother too.'

Moisture glistened in the farmer's sky-blue eyes and his tanned throat rose and fell over a tight swallow. 'I miss her too,' he said in a cracked voice. 'God knows, a day doesn't go past when I don't miss her.'

'Have you told Candi that?' Fran asked gently.

His jaw worked for a moment in an effort to gain self-control, his gaze dropping to his hat resting now against his thighs. 'No…' He cleared his throat. 'No. I haven't.' He looked at her again, his eyes brimming with tears. 'You reckon I should?'

Fran nodded. 'I think it's time. She needs to know she's not the only one who has lost someone she loved dearly. Maybe she needs to see how hard it is for you. Perhaps she has misinterpreted your strength and stoicism for not caring enough.'

He brushed at his eyes with the back of his hand. 'I reckon you're right. I've always been a stiff-upper-lip sort of guy like my father. When my mother died he just carried on as if it was another day on the farm. I guess I thought that was the best way to handle things.'

'You're doing the best you can do, Jim, so don't beat yourself up about making mistakes occasionally,' Fran said. 'You're human and have feelings and emotions just like your daughter does. I'll drop out to see Candi if you like. When would be a good time?'

His face brightened. 'You'd do that?'

She smiled. 'Of course.'

He ran his fingers over the rim of his acubra hat. 'Give me a day or two to talk to her, you know…about her mother.' He looked up again. 'What about Sunday, say, three in the afternoon?'

'I'll look forward to it.'

Jim scuffed his booted feet, shifting his lean body awkwardly, as if he was still not sure where to carry the emotion that had risen to the surface. He stretched out his work-roughened hand and gripped Fran's firmly. 'Thank you, for everything. I wish you were the doctor taking on the position. I can't think of anyone more suitable for this place.'

Fran pushed aside her guilt with even more force. 'I'm sure the new locum will be perfect. I'll see you on Sunday.'

She let out her breath once the farmer had gone and continued on her way across the street to Tony's Milk Bar. She sat in one of the old-fashioned booths and sipped her cup of tea as she waited for her sandwich to be prepared, watching as the heat haze shimmered on the street outside.

The bell above the door of the milk bar pinged as it opened and Fran looked up to see Jacob come in. He took off his police hat and smiled at her. 'Hi.'

'Hi…'

'G'day, Sarg,' Tony said from behind the counter. 'What'll you have?'

'Just a flat white, thanks, Tony.'

'Sure I can't make you a steak sandwich? Or what about a burger?'

'Not today. I've only got a minute or two. The coffee will be fine.'

'Coming right up.'

Fran felt the brush of Jacob's knees against hers as he sat in the opposite seat of the booth. She felt her whole body spring to life, the blood rushing through her veins.

'Hot enough for you?' he asked, a secret message in his gaze.

'I've decided I like it hot,' she said. 'I like it a lot.'

He leaned his forearms on the table, his hands within touching distance of hers. Fran looked down at his fingers; she had only to move hers a couple of centimetres to make contact. She was just about to inch forward to do so when he spoke.

'I've been thinking,' he said. 'We should try and keep this thing between us between ourselves and not the whole of Pelican Bay for as long as we can.'

Fran hoped the disappointment she felt wasn't showing on her face. She wanted to shout how she felt about him from the top of the gumtrees but he clearly wanted to keep things quiet. She understood that. He was a high-profile person in a small community. But a part of her wanted him to openly acknowledge her as his girlfriend.

'Probably a good idea,' she said, glad now she hadn't phoned her sister and blurted out her happiness.

Jacob glanced at Tony, who was coming across with a coffee in one hand and Fran's salad sandwich on a plate with a neatly folded paper napkin in the other. Jacob leaned back in the booth as Tony put the food and drink on the table.

'Anything else I can get you?' Tony asked.

'No, thank you,' Fran said. 'This is lovely.'

Tony looked at Jacob. 'I heard on the news they caught that guy that did over Wade Smith.'

'Yeah,' Jacob said, stirring his coffee. 'That's what I came in to tell Dr Nin.'

Fran felt her shoulders drop a little further. This was business, not personal. She would have to learn the difference, and quickly.

'Anyone we know?' Tony asked.

Jacob shifted his mouth in a negative gesture. 'No, it wasn't a local. Smith had a run-in with an associate from his time in prison. The guy drove down here, got into an argument and things turned nasty. He made it look like a hit and run so no one would connect him, but his DNA was all over Smith's place and Smith's DNA and blood were in the back of his car. Smith woke up late last night and confirmed who attacked him.'

After a few more words about the case Tony went back to the kitchen. Jacob drained the contents of his cup and set it back down on its saucer.

'It must be very satisfying for you to have solved the case,' Fran said.

'It was a team effort,' he said. 'But, yes, it is satisfying. It's one of the reasons I love being a cop. You can't solve every case but you can keep on trying. Take my father's murder, for instance. I might never get the closure I want on that but it's not going to keep me from having a damn good go at it.'

Fran reached for his hand and was deeply touched he didn't pull away. 'I think your dad would be immensely proud of you, Jacob,' she said softly.

'Thank you,' he said, turning over her hand and giving it a little squeeze. 'I'd better get going.' He reached for his hat on the bench seat. 'Are you planning on coming around this evening for a workout before dinner?'

Fran wished she had the strength to say no. Perhaps playing a little harder to get would make him less reluctant to keep their relationship private, but she was not a manipulator by nature and didn't intend to start now. 'That would be great, if it's OK with you?'

His fingers brushed against hers in a fleeting caress as he slid out of the booth. 'I'm counting the hours,' he said. Placing his hat on his head, he winked at her and left.

After he had disappeared from sight Fran looked down at her untouched sandwich. Her stomach was twitching with excitement, not hunger. She could barely draw in a breath without feeling as if it was snagging on something deep inside.

'Lost your appetite, Dr Nin?' Tony asked as he came past to collect Jacob's used cup.

'Um…I…'

He grinned at her. 'You and Sergeant Hawke will give my place a bad name if you don't eat when you meet in here.'

'Oh, we weren't meeting…you know, as in meeting like on a date or something.' Fran felt the words tumbling out of her mouth, her face firing up the more she said, so she stopped before she did any more damage.

'Yeah, and I believe you.' Tony scooped up her plate with a knowing look. 'I'll wrap this to go. Maybe you'll feel like it later.'

Fran gave him a pasted-on smile. 'Thanks. I'm sure I will.'

As Fran was making her way back home she ran into Tara, who was on her way to start her shift at the store. She was showing a little less stress and even discussed attending school a little more regularly.

'I don't want to work in a shop for the rest of my life,' Tara explained. 'I mean, not unless I owned it.'

'Have you thought about what you would like to do when you leave school?' Fran asked.

Tara pushed down her sleeves as if she wanted to put the past out of sight. 'Yes,' she said with a spark of determination in her eyes. 'I want to be a doctor. A GP, just like you.'

'Actually, I'm not—' Fran stopped, thought a bit and then continued, 'I trained as an A and E specialist.'

'So why'd you change to being a GP?'

'I didn't change...' Fran said, feeling tongue-tied and awkward.

'But you're a great GP,' Tara said. 'I would love it if you stayed here.'

'I'm afraid that's not possible,' Fran said as firmly as she could.

'But why?'

She told Tara a little about what had happened, keeping the worst of it to herself rather than put off the young girl's aspiration to be a doctor. 'So I ended up quite by chance here in Pelican Bay for that one session,' she concluded.

'Wow, that's way cool,' Tara said. 'Like, what would have happened to me if you hadn't come along at exactly the right time? You really helped me the other day, you know? I did some thinking when I went home. I've been kind of letting my mother win by allowing her desertion to screw up my life. But I don't want my life to be like that any more. I want to help people like you do every day. I want my life to count for something.'

Fran felt a slowly spreading warmth flow into every hollow space in her chest. 'I'm so happy for you, Tara. I think you will be great at whatever you decide to do.'

Tara beamed. 'Is it OK if I bring my brother Sam with me on one our walks?'

'Sure it is,' Fran said. 'I'm looking forward to meeting him.'

'I just have to convince him to come.' Tara gave her a woman-to-woman look. 'You know what guys are like.'

'I sure do,' Fran said with feeling.

Tara shifted her weight from foot to foot. 'Um…I want to thank you for what you did for my father, you know…speaking to Sergeant Hawke?'

'Oh… Right…well, I hope… I mean I'm sure Sergeant Hawke's not going to make a fuss or anything.'

'He came to our house.'

Fran lifted her brows. 'Oh?'

Tara nodded. 'He brought around a six-pack of beer for my dad. They had a long chat. Sergeant Hawke organised some sort of hire purchase thing with Joe Pelleri so Dad can get some new tyres for his car. Mr Pelleri's giving him a big discount but to tell you the truth I think Sergeant Hawke put him up to it.'

Fran felt that spreading warmth inside again. 'It certainly sounds like something Sergeant Hawke would do.'

'He's a very private sort of guy, isn't he?'

'Sergeant Hawke, you mean?'

Tara gave a little nod. 'He likes to keep it quiet about all the good stuff he does for people around here. I like that about him. He's not up himself, like a lot of guys I know. I think it's great you and he are seeing each other. It'd be totally cool if you two got married and stayed here for ever.'

Fran blinked. 'Um…we're not…I mean…it's not…' She trailed off helplessly.

'I saw you at the milk bar just now,' Tara said. 'I hope

someday a gorgeous man will look at me like that, you know, with eyes that sort of melt.'

Fran swallowed. 'Um…it's not really what you think…'

Tara smiled as she hauled her backpack back over one shoulder. 'I'd better get going. I told Mrs Hadley I would do an extra shift for her at the store. I'll call you about a walk with Sam some time early next week. I reckon it will take me the rest of the week and the weekend to bribe him into coming.'

Before Fran left for Jacob's house she took Rufus for a walk along the beach. There was an onshore breeze that filled the air with sea spray and carried the lonely cries of a pair of pied oyster-catchers towards her. She pulled back her hair and tied it around itself like a loosely knotted rope, lifting her face to the briny air and breathing in its refreshing coolness after the brooding heat of the day.

Rufus gave a happy bark and bolted off. Fran blinked her eyes open to see him wag his tail at Jacob, who had come through the bush just a short distance ahead.

She watched as man and dog came towards her, Rufus leaping up and down with the sort of joy she was feeling inside at the sight of the man she loved. She ached to be able to tell him but it was far too soon to be saying those three little words. She had discussed with friends many times how men these days were hesitant to commit. They liked their freedom too much. Marriage and babies were things they put off until their thirties, sometimes later, and sometimes they chose not to go down that pathway at all.

Fran couldn't imagine going through life without a family to cherish. She had dreamed of it all her life. Her own loving background was something she wanted to re-create for herself. She had watched her mother continue to blossom under her father's love. For close to thirty-five years they had been a solid and devoted couple who were so well balanced both Fran and her sister had vowed from an early age they were not going to settle for a man who wasn't completely committed to them.

'Hi,' Jacob said, coming to stand in front of her. 'I thought I might find you down here.'

'It's my favourite place,' she said, smiling at him.

He lifted his hand and brushed a wispy strand of her hair back from her face where it had come loose from its make-shift ponytail. He watched as her pupils dilated and how the tip of her tongue sneaked out to moisten her lips. He felt that familiar punch in his gut of raw attraction, his lower body pulsing with the need to bury himself in her again. She was at her most beautiful like this, barefoot on the beach, hair all over the place, her cheeks slightly flushed and that cute flicker of uncertainty in her eyes every time they came in contact with his.

He closed the distance between their bodies and tilted her face upwards to receive his mouth. She tasted of sea spray and strawberry lipgloss and he felt as if he could never have enough of her. His tongue found hers and a lightning zap of red-hot desire shot right through him. He instantly hardened, the throb of blood a tight ache that made him want to push her to the sand at their feet and plunge into her silky warmth.

She pressed herself against him, her slim form fitting perfectly along the hard ridges and planes of his body. His hands went to the small of her back and brought her that little bit closer. He felt her slim pelvis quiver at the contact and heard her soft breathless gasp as he moved his mouth to the sensitive skin of her neck. 'Do you have any idea how much I want you?' he asked as he moved his way down to the delicate scaffold of her collarbones.

'Um…pretty much,' she said in a soft voice just shy of a whisper.

He cupped her face in his hands, looking into her eyes as the sea raged and pounded at the shore behind him, while his blood raged and pounded inside him. 'I don't think I have ever wanted someone like I want you,' he said. 'I know you probably think that's a line or something, but it's true. I haven't felt like this before.'

She smiled a smile that lit up her grey-blue eyes. 'Wow.'

He gave her a mock frown. 'Is that all you can say?'

She let out a dreamy sigh. 'Oh, wow…'

He smiled and, leaning down again, brushed her mouth with his. 'I promised you dinner last night and reneged on the deal. This time I promise I'm not going to make love to you until I have fed you first.'

'I hope you haven't gone to any trouble,' Fran said as they walked back the way she had come.

'I had a bit of help from Beryl,' he said with a sheepish smile.

She raised her brows at him. 'Does Beryl know who you have invited to dinner?'

'I think she's made a fairly accurate guess.' He stopped, bent down and, picking up a piece of driftwood, threw it well ahead for Rufus.

Fran chewed at her lip for a few more steps before she asked, 'I think more people than you realise already know about us.' She stopped and looked up at him. 'Tara, for instance, saw us at Tony's. And Tony himself hinted at it after you left.'

He shrugged and, capturing her hand, pressed a kiss to her

fingertips. 'It's one of the down sides of living in a small community. You only have to look at someone and the gossip starts like wildfire. I try to ignore most of it but now and again it gets to me.'

Fran hoped it wouldn't affect them. As new as their relationship was, she knew she would be gutted if it ended before it had a chance to grow. Her whole being responded to him, she could even feel the pulse of her blood in her fingertips where his lips had so briefly rested.

They were almost at the path to Fran's sister's house when Jacob's mobile phone rang. He grimaced as he checked the screen. 'This looks like trouble,' he said to her before he answered it.

Fran couldn't help but hear snatches of the conversation. Her heart began to pound with dread as Nathan Jeffrey reported an incident out at the Bellbird Gully quarry, just called in by a neighbour.

'Right, I'll head out there now,' Jacob told him. 'I'll take Dr Nin with me in case there is any delay with the ambulance.'

He ended the call and gave Fran a grim look. 'Looks like Beth Judd's been hurt. It sounds serious. She was found unconscious near the clothesline.'

'Where's Kane?' Fran asked, her stomach churning with cold hard stones of dread.

Jacob's expression made the stones roll in her stomach all the more. 'There's no sign of the child or the boyfriend.'

Fran swallowed tightly as she hurried to get her doctor's bag. She came back out after locking Rufus in the house and joined Jacob who already had the engine running of the police vehicle he had parked behind her car before he had met her down on the beach.

It was a harrowing few minutes as they drove to the cottage

near the deserted quarry where Beth Judd and Dave Calder lived. Fran berated herself all the way, furious that she hadn't done something about the situation from the get-go.

She ran her tongue over her panic-dry lips. 'Does anyone have any idea if Dave might have taken Kane?'

Jacob glanced at her as he took the turn to Bellbird Gully, his expression dark. 'No one knows.'

She pressed her lips together, only releasing them to say, 'This is my fault. If something happens to one of them, it will be my fault.'

He put his foot down even harder on the accelerator as he steered the car up the rough driveway to the cottage. 'No, it's not, Fran. We'll make sure we do everything we can.'

Fran took a steadying breath, trying to find some comfort in his words, but there was none.

CHAPTER ELEVEN

WHEN they finally got to the rundown cottage perched on a steep hill next to the old quarry site, the neighbour was standing helplessly near the clothesline where Beth was lying on her back next to a basket of wet laundry, unconscious.

Beth was breathing normally, but her pulse was racing at over 100. There were no obvious cuts and abrasions other than an ugly bruise on one side of her face that looked as if it was a day or so old. Fran checked Beth's pupils—the right was larger than the left, suggestive of a head injury. She examined Beth's head, particularly the back of the skull, but there was no sign of any injury—no swelling, no blood and no bleeding from the ears or nose.

'How is she?' Jacob asked as he came over once he'd taken a quick statement from the neighbour.

'She's breathing normally,' she said, reaching for her stethoscope. 'I can't find any external sign of head injury but that's not to say she hasn't got one—one of her pupils is dilated.'

'The ambulance is about twenty minutes away,' he said, looking at the clothes basket and the scattered bucket of pegs on the ground, a frown of concentration bringing his brows together. 'Apparently there was a mix-up with the volunteer roster.'

Fran mentally rolled her eyes as she listened to Beth's strong and steady heartbeat. She pulled the earpieces of the stethoscope out of her ears and looked across at Jacob, who was crouched under the clothesline, looking at the dusty ground.

'Any news on Dave and Kane's whereabouts?' she asked.

'Nathan Jeffrey is working on finding him as we speak,' he said, straightening. 'Apparently he had today off work. One of his workmates said he'd mentioned something about going fishing.'

Jacob swept his narrowed gaze across the sun-scorched area surrounding the old cottage. 'I'm going to take a look around. Call me if you need me.'

Fran murmured something in response as she smoothed Beth's clothing back over her.

Beth opened her eyes. 'W-what's going on?'

'Beth, you were found unconscious by your neighbour out here,' Fran explained.

Beth blinked her eyes a couple of times, her expression confused. 'Where's Kane? I…I had him with me when I was hanging out the clothes.'

'Doesn't Dave have Kane with him?' Fran asked.

Beth blinked again, as if trying to remember. 'No…why should he? I told you: he was with me while I was hanging out the washing.' She struggled to get up but her face went chalk-white. 'Oh, God, where's my baby?'

Fran felt her heart start to knock like a swinging hammer in her chest. 'Beth, are you absolutely *sure* Kane was with you all the time?'

Beth's mouth was trembling uncontrollably as she grasped at Fran's hand. 'Help me… Oh, God, help me…'

Fran squeezed Beth's hand. 'We're doing all we can, Beth. The ambulance is on its way. You'll need to go to hospital to—'

Beth struggled to get up. 'I'm not going to hospital. I'm not sick. You can't make me. I have to find Kane. Don't you understand?' Her eyes were wild with panic. 'I have to find my baby!'

'Beth, what happened? Is this anything to do with Dave? There's help and support available. You don't have to go through this any more.'

Beth screwed up her face in a frown. 'What are you talking about? Dave didn't hit me. You think Dave hurt Kane? How dare you spread such untruths?'

'Beth, I'm not suggesting anything. We're just trying to find out what happened. What about little Kane's arm?' Fran asked.

Beth flopped back down as if in defeat. 'He didn't hit me or Kane…'

Fran glanced at the area beneath the clothesline Jacob had been studying so intently earlier. There were the tiny footprints of Kane and the narrow prints of what appeared to be Beth's shoes, as well as the tiny tyre marks of a toy truck. There was no sign of a scuffle.

Fran's thoughts began to run through various scenarios.

She turned back to Beth. 'Beth, what's the last thing you can recall before you woke up just now?'

Beth blinked again as if to clear her dazed mind. 'I was carrying out the washing… Kane had his tip truck with him. He stopped to look down at a beetle on the ground. I told him it was a Christmas beetle and then…' She swallowed and gave Fran a hollow-eyed look. 'And then I blacked out.'

Fran stroked the sweaty hair back from Beth's brow. 'Has that ever happened before?'

Beth bit her bottom lip until it went white. 'Yes…' She began to cry. 'I dropped Kane the first time…you know when his arm got injured? I was so scared someone would take him off me. My mother threatened to do it when she heard I was involved with Dave. Somehow she heard how he'd been in youth detention in the past.'

'It's all right, Beth,' Fran said gently. 'No one's going to take Kane away from you. Tell me about what happened to your face. You have a nasty bruise that looks about a day or so old. Do you remember anything about how you got that?'

'I had another blackout. It happened when Dave was out in the back garden with Kane. I hit my face on the edge of the kitchen table as I went down. Dave found me just as I was coming to…'

Fran leaned closer to Beth. 'Beth, I think we'll have to take you to hospital to do a CAT scan. Something must be causing these blackouts—we need to find out what it is.'

Beth's eyes went wide with shock. 'Brain cancer?'

'That's very unlikely—brain tumours are rare. It's most likely we'll find something that's fixable. But we have to do the tests.'

'But what will happen to Kane if I go to hospital?'

'Social services will do all they can to make sure he is well looked after if you feel Dave would not be able to cope.'

Beth's eyes streamed with tears again. 'I don't want to put too much stress on Dave. He's been so good to me and Kane. He's still finding his feet with handling a little kid. It's a lot to ask of him.'

'Do you know where he is right now?' Jacob asked as he came back. 'We need to tell him what's happened to you and to find out where Kane is.'

Beth screwed up her eyes as if the sunlight hurt her.

'He had the day off today. He wanted to take Kane and me

fishing but I always get seasick.' She bit her lip again. 'We're short of money…I guess you can sort of tell by the look of this place. It's all we can afford. He goes fishing at least twice a week so we have something to eat—meat is so expensive.'

Fran stroked Beth's thin hand. 'Times are tough on a lot of young people starting out,' she said. 'We'll make sure he's found as soon as possible and brought to the hospital to see you.'

The ambulance struggled up the drive, closely followed by a police vehicle containing two officers, the young fresh-faced Constable Jeffrey and the other a senior constable. Jacob quickly filled his colleagues in while Fran helped as Beth was loaded into the ambulance.

'Hold that ambulance,' Jacob commanded as he began to follow some track marks in the dust leading to the quarry. 'Don't let it leave until we have conducted a thorough search.'

Fran joined in the search under Jacob's direction, taking measured steps, her gaze covering the small area he had allotted her. The bush was scraggly and the air was hot with a breeze that carried particles of dust from the abandoned quarry a few hundred metres from where she was searching. The ground was much less rocky in her area, and she wondered if Jacob had done that deliberately, to keep her leg from being stretched beyond its current capacity. She could see he had taken the most dangerous section to search, the deep quarry with its rocky broken jaws gaping like a grotesque mouth waiting for something to devour.

Fran paused for a moment to listen, as Jacob had instructed her earlier, but this time she heard a faint whimper. She walked towards the noise, cocking her head, wondering if she was imagining it. She was about to call out to Jacob to tell him she thought she had heard something when she saw the black hole of a mineshaft partially covered by scrub. She quickly stepped backwards but her weak leg couldn't hold her. It folded beneath her and, landing awkwardly and heavily, she felt the ground fall away as if in slow motion.

'Fran!' Jacob's voice sounded like a muffled canon as she went down. She was falling, falling, falling, and by some miracle she opened her eyes in time to see a tree root, like a gnarled ghostly finger reaching out for her to grasp. She reached for it almost blindly, dust and debris clouding her vision. She hung there, like a rag doll, her head spinning, her body aching, adrenalin surging through her.

It was then she heard the same tiny whimper she had heard before. She tightened her hold on the root and looked below to where there was a ledge about an arm's length away. Kane's little body was lying in a crumpled heap, dust-covered, blood-streaked but thankfully alive. He opened his little mouth and wailed, 'Mummy!'

'It's all right, darling,' Fran said, desperately trying not to cry in case it traumatised him further. 'Mummy sent me to get you.'

'I felled down,' he wailed, and began to scramble to his feet.

'Don't move!' Jacob's voice rang out, echoing eerily off the mineshaft walls. 'For God's sake, don't either of you move.'

Fran felt her blood run cold as she finally realised the danger she and Kane were in. She had never felt so frightened. If Scott Draper and his drug-induced rage faced her now, she would have brushed him off like a fly.

This was life and death.

She would never forgive herself if she let Kane fall to his death, as he most certainly would if he fell further. She had no idea how deep the shaft was, but even with the light coming down from the scrub Jacob had pulled back it seemed bottomless. The ledge Kane was on would not tolerate any further weight, and Fran had already felt the tree root she was clinging to tremble as if it was going to give way.

'I'm going to send down a rope.' Jacob spoke with calm authority from above. 'I want you to double it around your waist and then carefully reach out to Kane. Don't make any sudden moves.'

Fran felt her bottom lip quiver as the rope snaked down to swing before her. 'I'm s-scared,' she said, just loud enough for Jacob to hear.

'You're doing great, sweetheart,' he said, smiling down at her. 'You're doing just great, baby. Now, if you can wind the rope around your waist, yeah, that's my girl. Now…slowly reach down for Kane.'

Fran did as he directed, even though her hands were shaking uncontrollably. Kane looked up at her, his dust-streaked face so endearing and hopeful she felt tears well up in her eyes. 'I'm coming, baby,' she said. 'I'm coming.'

She leaned down to reach him, her body supported by the rope, her fingers brushing the child's but not quite connecting. 'Reach up for me, Kane,' she said. 'We're going to see Mummy, OK?'

'My twuck's falled down,' he said, pointing to the black unblinking eye of the mineshaft below him.

Fran felt her heart lurch at the same time her body swung out against the rockface as the tree root broke off, banging her against the side of the narrow shaft, making her feel every bump and ridge against her flesh. 'I'll buy you a new one, darling,' she promised as she reached for him again. 'I'll buy you a hundred new ones. Come on, sweetie, take my hand. *Come on!*'

'I want my twuck!' the little boy wailed again.

There was the sound of footsteps rapidly approaching and a young man's voice called out. 'Kane? It's Dave.'

Fran glanced up to the column of sunlight to see the ashen face of a man not much older than Beth looking down at her and Kane, the senior police officer holding him back from the edge.

'Careful, mate,' the officer said. 'We don't want three of you down there.'

'You gotta get him up,' Dave said, looking at Jacob in desperation.

'We'll get him up, don't worry,' Jacob said, although Fran could hear the strain in his voice.

Dave knelt down so he could speak to Kane. 'Kane, listen to me, mate. You reach up for the pretty lady's hand, OK? We gonna go shopping for the biggest tip truck you ever did see once you're out of there, I promise.'

Kane slowly raised his little hand towards Fran's. The feel of those tiny chubby fingers encased in her slim ones was something she knew she would never forget, not if she lived for a hundred years. She felt like laughing out loud as she and Kane were drawn up to safety.

She was bruised, she was battered, she had dust in places she didn't want to think about, but they were safe. Kane was being hugged by Dave, who was crying unashamedly, saying repeatedly, 'It's all right, Daddy Dave's here now.' And Fran was crying, for the simple joy of being alive. What did it matter that she had a permanent limp? She'd still been able to rescue an infant from a mineshaft ledge no one else present would have been able to reach, given their broad-shouldered builds.

Jacob reached for her as someone else led Kane and Dave

towards the waiting ambulance. 'Don't you ever do that to me again,' he said as he held her so close to him she felt she was being crushed. 'I thought I was going to lose you. I couldn't bear to lose you, not when I've only just found you.'

Fran kept holding on to him, breathing in his scent, marvelling at how sure she felt about her feelings for him. It seemed the perfect time to tell him. She pulled back in his hold and looked at his dusty and reddened eyes. 'Hey, I think I love you,' she said.

He was still breathing heavily, his chest moving up and down against hers. 'Did you have to go falling into a mineshaft to come to that conclusion?' he asked.

She grinned at him. 'You know something? I think I did, yes.'

'My life flashed before my eyes when you disappeared down that hole,' he said in a ragged tone. 'It was then I realised I couldn't bear to go on without you in it. I know you don't want to stay in Pelican Bay. I'm not going to pressure you to do anything you don't feel up to doing, but please think about staying here as my wife.'

Fran blinked her eyes a couple of times. 'Did you just propose to me?'

Jacob laughed. 'Yeah, I think I just did. How long have we known each other?'

'A couple of weeks.'

'Long enough.'

She widened her eyes. 'You think?'

'My mother told me just before she died that she knew she was going to marry my father the first time she met him.'

'Where did you meet him?' Fran asked.

'He nearly ran her down with his motorbike,' he said with a crooked grin.

'Oh, well, then, it looks like this was meant to be,' Fran

said, still grinning from ear to ear. 'Caro will be beside herself. No, actually, she'll probably be annoyed that she didn't have something to do with getting us together. She's been husband-hunting for years for me to no avail.'

Jacob gathered her close again. 'No pressure, sweetheart, but I just heard from one of the ambos that the doctor they had lined up for the locum has some issues with his overseas qualifications. It could be a while before they find a replacement. Do you think you could step up to the plate in the meantime?'

Fran looked up at him with adoration. 'How long do you think it will take to find a new locum?'

He gave her a sexy grin. 'What say we give it nine months at least, then instead of claiming a headache you can give the patients a genuine excuse for calling off consultations.'

Fran smiled radiantly as she nestled up close. 'At least then if I have to cancel a clinic at short notice, I can honestly say it's your fault.'

He brought his mouth down to just above hers. 'I can't wait until I am proven guilty,' he said, and kissed her until they were both breathless.

Two months later

When Fran arrived at the Pelican Bay church on her father's arm it seemed the whole town had turned up. All the familiar faces were there—Candi and her father, the Pelleri family, and Tara and Sam Clark with their father Wayne. Kane was being held by Dave with one hand, the other arm protectively around the waist of Beth, her hair only just starting to grow back after her surgery for a benign tumour.

The collective sigh as Fran walked down the aisle towards

the tall figure of Jacob made her skin tighten with excitement. He was smiling at her, his blue eyes glistening with moisture the closer she got.

Caro, as matron of honour, was blubbering, their mother stalwartly and surreptitiously feeding her tissues from the front pew.

'You look breathtakingly beautiful,' Jacob said as Fran came to stand beside him.

She smiled up at him. 'You look pretty amazing yourself.'

He squeezed her hands in his. 'Everyone in town is here. That is how much everyone adores you.'

'Not quite everyone,' Fran whispered back. 'Rufus is back at the house with a juicy bone.'

Jacob's eyes twinkled. 'Are you absolutely sure about that?'

She turned as she heard an all-too-familiar bark at the entrance to the church. Before anyone could do anything to stop him, Rufus came bolting down the aisle to sit at Jacob's feet, his tail thumping the floor excitedly.

Jacob reached down and unclipped a little parcel attached to Rufus's collar. 'Thanks, mate,' he said, giving the dog a quick ruffle of his ears.

Fran's eyes widened. 'You trusted him with the rings?'

Jacob grinned. 'Who else would I ask to be my best man?'

MEDICAL™ 2-in-1

Coming next month

EMERGENCY: PARENTS NEEDED
by Jessica Matthews

Paramedic Joe finds himself caring for a baby daughter he never knew existed, but what does a bachelor know about babies? Bubbly colleague Maggie must make this sinfully handsome man realise he *can* be a good father... and husband!

A BABY TO CARE FOR
by Lucy Clark

Orphaned newborn baby – stand-in mum needed: how can Outback paediatrician Iris refuse? Especially when local playboy Dr Dex Crawford offers to help! Falling for both man and baby, Iris hopes their temporary family can become full-time bliss...

PLAYBOY SURGEON, TOP-NOTCH DAD
by Janice Lynn

Single mum Blair guards her heart fiercely – especially against notorious playboys like her new boss, Dr Oz Manning. But might this beautiful nurse and her adorable little girl be the ones to turn this lovable rogue into a family man for ever...?

ONE SUMMER IN SANTA FE
by Molly Evans

Devoted to his patients, Taylor has managed to avoid emotional involvement, until he's blown away by his new temporary nurse. This dynamic doctor has one short summer to convince her to stay with him, permanently!

On sale 5ᵗʰ February 2010

 **MEDICAL**™

Single titles coming next month

ONE TINY MIRACLE...
by Carol Marinelli

Since losing his wife and unborn child, 'home' is just a word to doctor Ben. But disarming – and visibly pregnant – nurse Celeste captures Ben's heart and gives this damaged doctor a reason to smile again. Then Celeste's tiny miracle makes a premature arrival – is there a future for Ben right there by their sides?

MIDWIFE IN A MILLION
by Fiona McArthur

Ten years ago Kate abruptly called off her engagement to paramedic Rory, her childhood sweetheart. Now Rory's come home to finally ask her *why* she turned him down. When an Outback medical emergency forces them together, Kate and Rory must confront their past if they are to finally make a future – together...

On sale 5th February 2010

Available at WHSmith, Tesco, ASDA, Eason and all good bookshops.
For full Mills & Boon range including eBooks visit
www.millsandboon.co.uk

millsandboon.co.uk Community

Join Us!

The Community is the perfect place to meet and chat to kindred spirits who love books and reading as much as you do, but it's also the place to:

- **Get the inside scoop from authors about their latest books**
- **Learn how to write a romance book with advice from our editors**
- **Help us to continue publishing the best in women's fiction**
- **Share your thoughts on the books we publish**
- **Befriend other users**

Forums: Interact with each other as well as authors, editors and a whole host of other users worldwide.

Blogs: Every registered community member has their own blog to tell the world what they're up to and what's on their mind.

Book Challenge: We're aiming to read 5,000 books and have joined forces with The Reading Agency in our inaugural Book Challenge.

Profile Page: Showcase yourself and keep a record of your recent community activity.

Social Networking: We've added buttons at the end of every post to share via digg, Facebook, Google, Yahoo, technorati and de.licio.us.

www.millsandboon.co.uk

0110_M0ZED

2 FREE BOOKS
AND A SURPRISE GIFT

We would like to take this opportunity to thank you for reading this Mills & Boon® book by offering you the chance to take TWO more specially selected books from the Medical™ series absolutely FREE! We're also making this offer to introduce you to the benefits of the Mills & Boon® Book Club™—

- **FREE home delivery**
- **FREE gifts and competitions**
- **FREE monthly Newsletter**
- **Exclusive Mills & Boon Book Club offers**
- **Books available before they're in the shops**

Accepting these FREE books and gift places you under no obligation to buy, you may cancel at any time, even after receiving your free books. Simply complete your details below and return the entire page to the address below. You don't even need a stamp!

YES Please send me 2 free Medical books and a surprise gift. I understand that unless you hear from me, I will receive 5 superb new stories every month including two 2-in-1 books priced at £4.99 each and a single book priced at £3.19, postage and packing free. I am under no obligation to purchase any books and may cancel my subscription at any time. The free books and gift will be mine to keep in any case.

Ms/Mrs/Miss/Mr _____ Initials _____

_____

Surname _____

Address _____

_____

_____ Postcode _____

Send this whole page to: Mills & Boon Book Club, Free Book Offer, FREEPOST NAT 10298, Richmond, TW9 1BR

Offer valid in UK only and is not available to current Mills & Boon Book Club subscribers to this series. Overseas and Eire please write for details.. We reserve the right to refuse an application and applicants must be aged 18 years or over. Only one application per household. Terms and prices subject to change without notice. Offer expires 31st March 2010. As a result of this application, you may receive offers from Harlequin Mills & Boon and other carefully selected companies. If you would prefer not to share in this opportunity please write to The Data Manager, PO Box 676, Richmond, TW9 1WU.

Mills & Boon® is a registered trademark owned by Harlequin Mills & Boon Limited. Medical™ is being used as a trademark. The Mills & Boon® Book Club™ is being used as a trademark.